**“Molly, this is Dr. Williams.”**

All she could see was the top of what she assumed was a man’s head. She waited for her colleagues to part, not expecting them to reveal a familiar face.

“Theo!?”

She hadn’t seen him for four years but he looked just the same. Tall, close to six feet, with broad shoulders that belied his otherwise slim physique. His thick black hair, cut short at the sides, was swept away from his forehead above almond-shaped eyes that widened a little, the only indication that he was as surprised as she was.

“Hello, Molly. It’s been a while.” He nodded slightly but only managed a half smile. He didn’t look thrilled to see her and she couldn’t blame him.

Four years had passed but all of a sudden it seemed like yesterday.

She experienced the long-forgotten heat of embarrassment, could feel the blush creeping up her neck and into her face, and knew her cheeks were now stained pink.

She tried to school her features to mirror his. Pleasant surprise rather than abject mortification as she wished the floor would open up and swallow her.

Dear Reader,

Thank you for picking up this book—my 40th! I'm not sure that I ever imagined this number when I first put pen to paper, but it's been an incredible adventure, and I am so grateful to everyone who has read one or more of my novels.

My stories have been set everywhere from Antarctica to Canada, Hollywood to London, and Coober Pedy to Sydney, but this is the first one I've set in Byron Bay on Australia's east coast. Australia has such diverse landscapes, but the quintessential beachside locations are high on my list of favorites. Sun, surf, sand and sex are the perfect recipe for a romance, and summer in Byron was the perfect time and place for Molly and Theo to reconnect.

I'd love to hear from you if you've enjoyed this story or any of my others. You can visit my website, emilyforbesauthor.com, or drop me a line at emily@forbesau.com.

As always, happy reading.

*Emily*

# PREGNANCY SURPRISE IN BYRON BAY

EMILY FORBES

Recycling programs for this product may not exist in your area.

ISBN-13: 978-1-335-94248-7

Pregnancy Surprise in Byron Bay



For questions and comments about the quality of this book, please contact us at CustomerService@Harlequin.com.

Harlequin Enterprises ULC
22 Adelaide St. West, 41st Floor
Toronto, Ontario M5H 4E3, Canada
www.Harlequin.com

**Printed in U.S.A.**

**Emily Forbes** is an award-winning author of Medical Romance novels for Harlequin. She has written over thirty-five books and has twice been a finalist in the Australian Romantic Book of the Year Award, which she won in 2013 for her novel *Sydney Harbor Hospital: Bella's Wishlist*. You can get in touch with Emily at emily@forbesau.com, or visit her website at emily-forbesauthor.com.

**Books by Emily Forbes**

**Harlequin Medical Romance**

***A Sydney Central Reunion***

*Ali and the Rebel Doc*

***Bondi Beach Medics***

*Rescuing the Paramedic's Heart*
*A Gift to Change His Life*
*The Perfect Mother for His Son*
*Marriage Reunion in the ER*

***London Hospital Midwives***

*Reunited by Their Secret Daughter*

*Rescued by the Single Dad*
*Taming Her Hollywood Playboy*
*The Army Doc's Secret Princess*
*Rescued by the Australian GP*

Visit the Author Profile page
at Harlequin.com for more titles.

For Ned and Finn

In the time it has taken me to write forty books, you have grown from babies to young adults.
I am so proud of you both. You are amazing men: kind, intelligent, handsome, polite and funny.
You would both make fabulous heroes, and I hope you each get your own happily-ever-after one day.

All my love,
Mum

**Praise for**
**Emily Forbes**

"*Reunited by Their Secret Daughter* was a feel-good romance where the characters were destined to be together, their circumstances were extremely interesting, and which had a HEA magical enough for a fairy tale."

—*Harlequin Junkie*

# CHAPTER ONE

MOLLY PRESCOTT CHECKED the time as she stepped out of the surf at Clarkes Beach and picked up her towel. She cursed softly to herself. She'd need to hurry if she was going to make the meeting on time.

Who was she kidding? She was definitely going to be late, she thought as she dried her face and wiped her arms with her towel. The clinic manager, Paula, had organised a quick breakfast meeting to introduce everyone to the new locum doctor who was coming up from Sydney to provide cover in the Byron Bay clinic for a few weeks. But there would be enough staff for him or her to be introduced to until Molly arrived. She wasn't the most senior doctor on staff, she'd only been there for six months, and maybe no one would even notice if she was late. Or maybe they had come to expect it. Timekeeping was one thing she had difficulty with. She was always trying to squeeze too much into her day and time was constantly getting away from her as a result. It was a perpetual struggle. She hadn't won the battle yet but she hoped that one day she'd miraculously develop a time-management gene.

Punctuality had been one thing, along with resilience and independence, that she'd hoped might improve with her move to Byron Bay. Here in the northern New South Wales coastal town she had only a short commute to work—nothing like the fifty-minute trip she'd made twice a day back in Sydney—but instead of improving, she'd just filled that extra time with another activity—her daily swim.

She quickly towelled her blonde hair before throwing a T-shirt over her swimsuit and jogging up the beach. She still had to get home to the apartment she rented with Gemma, one of her colleagues, shower and then make the quarter of an hour walk from Lighthouse Road into town. She would have liked to have taken a detour past The Top Shop to grab some breakfast but she didn't have the extra ten minutes that would take.

She really should have cut her swim short today but it was her favourite way to start the day, she needed it for her mental health and it was an important part of the process of finding herself. Swimming gave her time to reflect on what she wanted out of life. After wasting years of her life with her ex-boyfriend, finally saying goodbye to Daniel was supposed to be a turning point in her life. Her plan had been to move to Byron Bay and to make time and space to work on herself. She no longer wanted to worry about pleasing others. She no longer wanted to seek attention. From her father. From her ex. From anyone.

She shook her head. She didn't want thoughts of Daniel encroaching on her mind. She was putting her past behind her, moving on from a bad relationship. Moving in general, she reminded herself as she checked her watch again, hoping her tardiness would be forgiven. Her consulting list didn't start until ten o'clock on Wednesdays so no one should expect her to be there at quarter to eight.

Molly's shoulder-length hair was still damp when she arrived at the clinic and she knew the humidity of the summer air would make it kink but she certainly couldn't have spared the time to blow-dry it. She sneaked into the staffroom a few minutes before eight, quite pleased with her effort, and relieved to hear Tom Reynolds, the senior doctor whose leave necessitated locum cover, still going around the room introducing the staff to the new locum.

She could smell coffee and she headed for the machine to grab a cup, along with a muffin, sending a silent thank you to Paula for organising food. She added milk to her coffee and took a bite of her muffin just as she heard Tom say, 'And, last but not least, is Dr Prescott.'

The room was full and many of the staff were standing, as there weren't enough chairs for everyone. Molly could hear Tom but, being only five feet four inches tall, she couldn't see to the front of the room. But Tom had obviously seen her tardy arrival.

She quickly tried to swallow the muffin and school her expression to casual nonchalance in an attempt to convey that she'd been at the back of the room all along as opposed to sneaking in thirty seconds before.

'Molly, this is Dr Williams.'

All she could see was the top of what she assumed was a man's head, although it could have been a tall woman. She waited for her colleagues to part, not expecting them to reveal a familiar face.

'Theo?'

She hadn't seen him for four years, but he looked just the same. Tall, close to six feet, with broad shoulders that belied his otherwise slim physique. His thick black hair, cut short at the sides, was swept away from his forehead above dark eyes that widened a little, the only indication that he was as surprised as she was.

'Hello, Molly. It's been a while.' He nodded slightly but only managed a half-smile. He didn't look all that thrilled to see her and she couldn't blame him.

Four years had passed but all of a sudden it felt like yesterday. And not in a good way.

She felt the long-forgotten heat of embarrassment, could feel the blush creeping up her neck and into her face, and knew her cheeks were now stained pink.

She tried to school her features to mirror his. Trying on a mask of pleasant surprise rather than abject embarrassment as she wished the floor would open up and swallow her.

She dropped her gaze, focusing on her coffee, as Tom continued speaking. She let her colleagues close the space and shield her from view as the colour faded in her cheeks.

'While I have you all here, I had a call from the organisers of Schoolies Festival. They need a few more volunteers for the weekend so if any of you can spare a few hours they'd love to hear from you. I think any clinical staff would be qualified to help, but, for any admin staff who are interested, as long as you have a police clearance and your first-aid accreditation, you can sign up too. Paula has the contact details.'

Her mind drifted as Tom continued speaking about the imminent influx of teenagers who would be descending on Byron Bay for the next ten days to celebrate the end of their school lives.

She threw her unfinished muffin into the rubbish, her appetite deserting her as the memories flooded in. She hadn't seen Theo since their university graduation ceremony and she hadn't spoken to him since they both attended the same party to celebrate the end of their final exams prior to graduation. The last words they'd exchanged had come just after she'd unceremoniously kissed him.

Mortified about her behaviour and still feeling the sting of rejection, she had avoided him at graduation as she'd tried to pretend nothing had happened. She'd been immensely relieved when he'd appeared reluctant to seek her out too.

But the feeling of embarrassment returned now as she remembered her foolishness. She knew she'd behaved badly. Drunk and emotional, she'd acted impulsively and then tried to pretend nothing had happened. Theo had treated her with kindness and compassion and she'd repaid his kindness with the assumption that he'd welcome her impulsive kiss, even though she'd been in a relationship. Albeit an emotionally complicated one.

He had kissed her back—she hadn't drunk so much that she'd forgotten that—but when he'd asked if she would take Daniel back if he had cheated on her she hadn't replied. She'd known she would. She'd done it every time. And Theo had known it too. He'd stood up and walked away.

She didn't want to be twenty-five again. She hadn't always made good choices four years ago but she had matured; life had a way of forcing you to grow up. She was rebuilding herself and she didn't really want to see someone who knew the old Molly, who knew the mistakes she'd made in the past, on a daily basis. Someone who she felt had judged her and found her lacking.

After four years she was still embarrassed and ashamed of her behaviour. Of the kiss. She'd acted carelessly and then realised she didn't want to be the girl who cheated on her boyfriend. She didn't want to be the cliché. Her boyfriend had cheated on her—often—but she didn't want to play tit for tat. She wanted to be the bigger person and kissing Theo had been a mistake. She shouldn't have put him in that position.

She could feel herself being watched and she lifted her eyes to see Gemma grinning at her from the other side of the room. Gemma raised her eyebrows, darted her eyes in Theo's direction and mouthed one word. *Wow.*

Molly glared at her and Gemma started to cross the room as Tom wrapped up the meeting and the rest of the staff began to disperse.

Molly had been vacillating over whether or not she should approach Theo. If she did, how should she behave? What should she say? Four years was a long time. Especially considering what had happened between them. So, at least Gemma's arrival meant she didn't have to make that decision. She could talk to Gemma instead. That would give her time to compose herself and work out how to manage this unexpected turn of events.

'Oh. My. God. Talk about tall, hot and handsome,' Gemma said as she reached Molly's side.

Molly glanced around, hoping Theo wasn't within earshot, and was relieved to find he'd actually left the room. She really didn't want to have this conversation with Gemma in the middle of the staffroom but it looked as though that was what she was getting.

'Where have you been hiding him?' Gemma asked.

'Theo?' Molly feigned indifference, knowing she felt anything but. 'I haven't been hiding him anywhere. I haven't seen him for years.'

Gemma was watching her closely. 'He's not a skeleton in your closet?'

Molly shook her head and turned away to gather the left-over breakfast items. Wrapping the platters of muffins and fruit and putting them into the fridge for later gave her an excuse to avoid Gemma's gaze as she tried to stop the blush from returning to her cheeks.

'So, you don't know if he's single?' Gemma continued.

Molly felt a twitch of jealousy. *Theo was hers.* But that was ridiculous. *She* was ridiculous. Gemma was quite entitled to fancy Theo.

'I have no idea, but I thought you were taking a break from dating?' she replied as she closed the fridge and started stacking empty coffee cups into the dishwasher.

Gemma had recently been dating a pilot but it turned out he had a girl in several cities and she was currently single. 'It only takes one man to change my mind. But tell me if he's off limits.'

'Why would he be off limits to you?' Molly

asked as she closed the dishwasher and switched it on.

'Several reasons. If you fancied him, for one. After all, you saw him first. Or if he's an ex of yours then I'm not going there.'

'I told you, he's not an ex. There's no history between us,' she said. She knew she was massaging the truth very slightly but she wasn't about to share all the embarrassing details. 'We studied together, that's all.'

'You've never mentioned him.'

'Why would I?'

'Because he's gorgeous and he works for Pacific Coast Clinics.'

'I didn't know he did.' She'd only been employed at the clinic for six months. She knew there were several associated clinics throughout New South Wales, and she knew the locum was coming from one of them, but she hadn't bothered to look at the staff list across all the different locations. There'd really been no need. 'You'll have to work fast—he's only here for six weeks,' Molly said, trying to sound light and breezy. It sounded like no time but Molly feared it might feel like an eternity.

'No.' Gemma shook her head. 'Looking like he does, I bet he's not single and I'm not going to get burned again.'

Molly didn't try and persuade her friend otherwise. Besides, she could be right, Theo could be spoken for already.

Molly wiped the bench, dried her hands and she and Gemma headed for their consulting rooms. She planned to use the extra time before her list started to follow up some of her patients, check their results and organise referrals. But her mind kept drifting.

She and Theo had studied medicine at university together but they hadn't been close friends. They'd moved in different circles. He'd spent a lot of his time in the library, she'd spent a lot of time in the university bar with Daniel, when they'd been 'on' again.

When their circles had overlapped she'd got the impression that Theo had judged her choices. She knew they'd been questionable but, at the time, her choices had made sense. At least in the world she knew.

She remembered Theo had a way of quietly watching people, taking stock, and once, in just a few moments, he had accurately summed up her and her relationship with Daniel, which had frustrated her. She hadn't wanted to hear his opinion. She'd wanted to be seen as strong and confident, not weak or scared, and she definitely hadn't wanted to admit that he'd been right.

There were so many things in her past she'd rather not think about. The present was about making better decisions. She was using her time in Byron Bay to find herself. To work on herself. She'd grown up, the middle of three sisters, always feeling as though her father would have preferred to have sons. She was constantly trying to prove that girls could do anything boys did, trying to be the perfect daughter. Then the perfect girlfriend. She'd been desperate for attention, desperate for affection.

She realised now that had been a big factor in her relationship with Daniel. Her father had ignored her mother, herself and her sisters and Molly had been flattered by Daniel's interest in her. He was intelligent, good-looking and popular and she'd been so desperate for attention she'd overlooked the negatives—his lies, his unfaithfulness, his unkindness. Her younger self had been happy just to have someone take notice of her and she knew she'd been conditioned to believe that everyone cheated—her father had certainly been guilty of the same offence on several occasions—and so the young Molly hadn't stopped to think about whether Daniel's attention was positive or negative. She hadn't cared. But not any more. She knew now that she didn't need someone else's validation—especially not when it was thinly-disguised emotional abuse. Now, away from her family and single for the first time in years, she was just trying to be the best version of herself. Whatever that was.

Here in Byron, she wasn't a sister, a daughter, a girlfriend. She was just Molly. A doctor. A friend.

But seeing Theo reminded her of the old Molly, the one she was trying to leave behind. She didn't want to be reminded of that girl.

She'd need to avoid Theo. And seeing as he was only in Byron Bay temporarily, it shouldn't be too hard.

Theo Chin Williams tried to concentrate as Tom Reynolds showed him around the clinic. He schooled his expression to make it look as if he was listening but he wasn't sure he would retain any of the information. His mind was too busy going back over old times. Back to Molly. He'd been stunned to see her at the clinic today. He hadn't seen her profile on the Pacific Coast Clinics website and he knew he would have noticed it, which meant it wasn't there. She must be new to the practice.

Four years was a long time but Molly hadn't changed. At least, not in appearance. She looked exactly the same—petite, blonde, shiny. Theo had always seen an aura of lightness and joy about her. With the exception of one memorable occasion, she'd always presented as a happy person. She'd been popular at university. She'd been fun and people had been drawn to her. He knew he had been. But they had mostly moved in different circles and Molly had barely noticed him. Except for that one night.

He remembered their last encounter. Their only intimate encounter in the seven years they'd been acquainted. Molly had cried on his shoulder, confided in him, kissed him and they hadn't spoken since.

He had admired her from afar for many years before that fateful night. He'd put her on a pedestal and hadn't been able to resist kissing her back when she'd abruptly and unexpectedly kissed him, but he'd been convinced she would never choose him over Daniel and so he'd walked away, wishing he were brave enough to stay.

At the end of the staff meeting he'd wondered if he should approach her, but what would he say after four years? They weren't friends, they were acquaintances at best. And then Tom had steered him out of the staffroom to embark on a tour of the clinic, taking the opportunity away from him.

Which brought his mind neatly back to the

matter at hand. Back to the reason he was in Byron Bay—to work. He was here for the next six weeks in a locum capacity but he'd also been tasked with some problem-solving. The Byron clinic was the newest addition to the Pacific Coast portfolio, a group of medical centres owned by his parents and managed by his mother, and she had flagged some issues, which Theo had been entrusted with sorting out. Between treating patients and going over the clinic's books and operating procedures he had enough on his plate. He didn't need to add Molly Prescott to his list. His mother was a perfectionist who expected nothing less than one hundred per cent effort at all times. He knew he was expected to return to Sydney with answers, and possibly solutions, to the issues she'd raised. He had plenty to focus on and his mother would not be pleased if he let himself get distracted. She wasn't interested in excuses, only in results.

Molly was a blast from the past but one that didn't need revisiting. He didn't need the distraction. Reminiscing wasn't a priority for him and he got the impression it wasn't high on her agenda either.

He forced himself to concentrate on the guided tour he was being given. He knew Tom's leave started today and he knew he would be expected to step up to the plate and take on a patient load immediately. He needed to focus. He hadn't seen Molly for four years. He could put her out of his mind for another few hours, at least while he was at work. He was older and wiser now, no longer infatuated. They had both moved on.

He could ignore the fact that she still glowed, still made the air around her shimmer. He could ignore the fact that his heart rate had escalated when their colleagues had parted to reveal her standing there and he could ignore the fact that his hands had perspired and his mouth had gone dry.

He could ignore her.

Molly scrolled through patients' test results on her computer screen but couldn't find the headspace to pick up the phone to pass any results on. She was being extremely unproductive. She was unsettled and she hated to admit it but Theo's arrival was responsible. She really thought she'd been making progress since she'd moved to Byron Bay. She was growing in confidence, no longer having to wonder what life with Daniel would have in store for her, whether she would be in or out of favour, whether she'd be fighting for attention or battling for his affection. She was on the path to independence and she didn't want Theo's arrival to pull her backwards. But she was stronger now, she wasn't the same girl any more, and she would show Theo that. Or just avoid him and allow him to see that for himself.

She nodded to herself, encouraged that she'd found a solution. She earmarked a couple of patients for the receptionists to call with non-urgent results and decided she'd go and grab another coffee before her consulting list started. Perhaps that would kick her brain into gear. Into the present and off the past.

On her way to the kitchen, she passed Paula's office. The practice manager had a large internal window looking out to the reception area. Molly glanced through the window and saw Theo leaning over Paula's desk, deep in conversation and pointing at a computer screen. What on earth could they be discussing? She paused briefly as her curiosity got the better of her, before realising she didn't want to be caught peering in at the unexpected tableau. It was none of her business and if it had been anyone but Theo she wouldn't have given it a second thought. Why did she find him so interesting?

Not wanting to go down that rabbit hole, she continued on to the kitchen but couldn't resist glancing through the window as she returned with her coffee. Theo was still there.

Molly kept walking and just as she reached the reception desk the front door to the clinic burst open and a very distressed middle-aged woman barrelled in, holding the door for her male partner. The man was overweight and sweating, not unusual in the humid air of Byron Bay, but Molly could see he was having difficulty breathing.

The woman plonked him on a seat and rushed to the desk, ignoring the other patients waiting to be attended to. 'Please, we need to see a doctor. My husband isn't well.'

'Are you a patient of the clinic?' the receptionist asked as Molly hurried around the desk and into the waiting room.

The woman shook her head. 'No. We're here on holiday. My husband has been complaining of indigestion, over-indulging I think, but it's got so bad this morning he's finding it hard to breathe.'

The clinic was not technically an emergency clinic but because they were right in the centre of town they got a lot of walk-ins. Despite the sign on the door giving the hospital's details, if the clinic was open people just turned up. The hospital had recently undergone extensive upgrades but, being a ten-minute drive out of town, it wasn't nearly as convenient. Especially for the tourists.

Molly sat down next to the man. 'My name is Molly, I'm one of the doctors.' He turned towards her but she could see he was having difficulty taking her words in. He was rubbing his sternum but it seemed to be an unconscious movement. 'Why don't you come with me and we'll get you looked at?' she continued.

She was concerned he was displaying symptoms of a cardiac episode. She could call for an ambulance but she knew from experience that dealing with any emergency was better done behind closed doors and out of the reception area. She wanted to get him somewhere with some privacy. He'd walked into the clinic, she just hoped he'd be able to walk into her consulting room. She didn't fancy her chances of breaking his fall if he toppled over.

'I'll take him, if you can get some details,' Molly told the receptionist.

The man stood, unsteadily, and Molly instinctively gave him her arm for support. 'What is your name?'

'Warwick,' he replied breathlessly.

Molly took him into the examination room where they had an ECG machine, just in case she needed it. She pressed on the footplate under the treatment bed, lowering it so Warwick could sit down. She lifted the back support and helped him to lift his feet.

'Can you describe to me what you're experiencing?'

'I'm having trouble breathing. It feels like someone is squeezing my lungs.'

'Does it hurt?'

Warwick nodded.

'Is this the first time you've had this pain?'

'It's the first time it's been this bad,' he said, not without some difficulty.

'Are you seeing a doctor for any chronic health conditions? Do you have any allergies? Any heart issues? Angina? Diabetes? Anxiety?'

Warwick shook his head.

'Are you taking any medications?' Molly asked as she wrapped a blood-pressure cuff around his arm and pressed the button to inflate it.

'Tablets for high cholesterol.'

Did he not think that was a condition worth mentioning? she thought as she looked at the reading on the monitor. She was surprised to find his blood pressure was within normal limits but noted his heart rate was rapid.

'I'd like to take a closer look at your heart. Have you ever had an ECG done before?'

Warwick shook his head again.

'I need to stick some electrodes onto your chest. Can you undo your shirt for me?' Molly asked as she turned her back to prepare the ECG machine.

'I don't…' Warwick's sentence faded away behind her. She spun around.

Warwick's eyes were closed. Was he breathing?

Molly looked for a rise and fall in his chest.

Nothing.

'Warwick?' She shook his shoulder before grabbing his wrist and feeling for a pulse.

Nothing.

She dropped the back of the bed, lying him flat.

She suspected he was in cardiac arrest.

She needed help.

She darted out of the room, snatching the defibrillator kit from the box on the wall outside Paula's office, and yelling instructions to Crystal at the reception desk as she flew past. 'Call an ambulance. Code blue.'

Through the window of Paula's office she could see Theo sitting by the desk.

She needed help and there was no time to go looking for it. She scanned the corridor, hoping someone else might materialise but, of course, no one did.

It would have to be Theo.

She stuck her head through the door. There was no time to worry about the past. She'd have to shelve her plans to avoid Theo.

She needed help.

She needed Theo.

'Theo!' She all but shouted his name, barely waiting for him to look up before she was already turning back to her exam room. 'I need you. Patient in cardiac arrest.'

## CHAPTER TWO

THEO LIFTED HIS head as he heard Molly call his name. She'd already turned on her heel and was heading along the passageway by the time he moved. As he stepped into the corridor, he was immediately enveloped by the scent of oranges hanging in the air and he was transported straight back to the night Molly had kissed him. Her hair had smelt of oranges then too. It was the scent of her shampoo. Now was not the time to be distracted, though. He hurried after her, catching up to her as she ducked into a clinic room. Her words trailed behind her. 'Middle-aged male, sudden cardiac arrest. No reported prior history.'

Theo nodded and said, 'I'll start compressions.' This wasn't how he'd imagined their first conversation would go but there was no time to waste. There was no time for the past.

Molly was avoiding eye contact, which piqued Theo's curiosity. Four years ago, they hadn't been friends, but they hadn't been enemies either—at least he hadn't thought so. But a cardiac event was a stressful situation. He couldn't expect her to spend time making him feel welcome.

Pushing his curiosity aside, he ripped open the buttons on the patient's shirt, exposing his chest and belly as Molly quickly opened the defibrillator kit and pulled out the pieces she needed. He leaned over the patient and placed his hands on his sternum, beginning chest compressions as Molly worked behind him.

Theo counted out loud and tried to ignore Molly as she moved around him. But it was difficult. She was hard to ignore. Each movement she made disturbed the orange-scented, perfumed air; he could feel where she was even when he couldn't see her. She squeezed behind him, putting her hands on his hips, obviously trying to keep him in position, trying not to disturb his rhythm, but her touch nearly made him lose track of his count.

'Fifteen.'

Molly's arm brushed his as she reached across to press the sticky pad onto Warwick's chest and a spark of awareness surged through him.

'Twenty.' His voice was husky. He cleared his throat and focused hard. Now was not the time to be thinking about Molly Prescott as anything more than his colleague.

He continued compressions as Molly placed the second pad onto the patient, this time without any further contact with Theo. She connected the pads to the machine and it began to issue instructions in its automated voice.

*'Stop CPR, analysing rhythm.'*

*'Shock advised.'*

Theo could hear the whine as the power built up in the defibrillator unit.

*'Stand clear.'*

'Clear.' Theo lifted his hands, holding them in the air, and repeated the machine's instructions. Molly stepped back from the bed and pressed the flashing red button. Theo stayed close. The patient was large and he was worried he could fall when the shock was delivered.

The patient lifted off the bed as the machine delivered a charge, trying to shock his heart out of fibrillation and restore its normal rhythm.

Theo and Molly waited but there was no change.

*'Continue CPR.'*

The machine continued its instructions.

'Are you okay to continue and I'll do the breaths?' Molly asked.

Theo nodded and resumed chest compressions. He knew the AED machine would expect two minutes of continued CPR before performing another analysis.

Molly opened the face-shield container and placed the shield over the patient's mouth and tipped his head back. Her left hand cupped his chin and Theo noticed her fingers were bare. She wasn't wearing a ring.

As Theo approached the count of thirty, Molly was preparing to give two breaths. Despite the fact they'd never worked together before their movements were smooth and coordinated. Theo reached thirty counts and paused and Molly bent her head and breathed into their patient. The transition from compressions to breaths was seamless.

Molly was standing opposite Theo now, keeping out of his way, and he watched the top of her head as she bent over the patient, her blonde hair falling over her face. She tossed her head to shift the hair from her eyes as she tilted her head to check for the accompanying rise of the patient's chest, making sure her breaths were reaching his lungs. Theo had to stop himself from reaching across and tucking Molly's hair behind her ear. He didn't think she'd appreciate the help but his fingers ached to touch her.

He returned his focus to his patient's chest

as Molly finished her second breath, making sure he wasn't caught looking at her when she straightened up.

They continued administering three more rounds of CPR. Two more long minutes before the machine interrupted them again.

*'Stop CPR, analysing rhythm.'*

*'Shock advised.'*

*'Stand clear.'*

Another jolt. But still nothing.

Theo continued with a fifth round of compressions. His shoulders were starting to complain—the patient was large and Theo was using a lot of effort, but he couldn't quit.

*'Analysing rhythm.'*

The defibrillator deliberated a possible third shock.

*'No shock advised.'*

*'Check pulse.'*

Molly checked for a pulse. 'I've got something!'

Her eyes met his. She was grinning, her smile was wide, full of relief and achievement, and Theo felt something tug at his heart. He smiled back. A proper smile this time, not the uncertain half-smile he'd bestowed on her earlier in the staff kitchen.

He let his hands drop and breathed out as Molly cried, 'We've got him!'

Theo could hardly believe it as the patient's eyes opened, a look of confusion on his face.

'Hello, Warwick.' Molly turned her attention to their patient and Theo felt a chill as her smile was directed at someone else. 'You gave us quite a scare.'

*Warwick.* That was the patient's name, Theo thought as Molly picked up the phone and buzzed the reception desk, asking Crystal to send the paramedics in when they arrived.

'We're going to send you off to hospital now and get you sorted out,' Molly continued as the door opened and Paula ushered the paramedics in, followed by a woman who Theo assumed was Warwick's wife. She made a beeline for their patient but Molly, who had her eyes trained on the woman, inclined her head slightly in Theo's direction. He understood her gesture—he needed to keep the wife out of the way while Molly did the patient handover. He steered the woman to a chair in the corner.

'Is he okay?' she asked. 'What happened? Why is the ambulance here?'

Theo didn't have much information but he had enough to pass on to the wife and hopefully ease her concerns.

'He's all right now but he needs to go to hospital.'

'For indigestion?' The woman was frowning.

'He went into cardiac arrest,' Theo explained gently. 'Your husband's heart stopped. We had to resuscitate him. He needs to go to hospital and he'll need further tests done.'

'He had a heart attack?'

'Cardiac arrest,' Theo repeated. 'It's a bit different from a heart attack.' Technically they were two different things but he didn't have time to go into that detail and he doubted if she'd remember much of what he told her anyway. 'Warwick will be seen by a cardiologist. They'll be able to give you more information.'

In his peripheral vision Theo could see the paramedics slipping an oxygen mask over Warwick's face as Molly took a final blood-pressure reading and removed the sticky pads from his chest. Warwick was transferred to the paramedics' stretcher as Molly removed the cuff.

'Can I go to the hospital with him?' Warwick's wife asked.

'Of course.'

Molly and Theo remained behind as the paramedics wheeled the stretcher out, followed by Warwick's wife.

Theo went to the sink in the corner and filled

two disposable cups with water. He handed one to Molly as she sat on the edge of the bed and let out a large sigh of relief.

'Thank you,' she said as she took the cup from him.

'Are you okay?' he asked.

She nodded. 'You?'

He smiled. 'Yep. Can't say I was expecting that on my first day though. Is Warwick a patient of yours?'

Molly shook her head. 'I've never seen him before. They're tourists, here on holiday.'

Theo frowned. 'But there's a hospital in Byron Bay. Why did they come here?'

Molly sipped her water. 'It happens a lot. We're in the centre of town. We're a lot more convenient.'

'But you're not an emergency clinic.'

'I know. But they thought it was indigestion.'

Theo wondered how often this occurred and what impact it had on the practice. On the staff. GPs weren't emergency physicians and the clinic certainly wasn't equipped like a hospital ED. Warwick had been lucky today.

'Warwick was lucky you knew what you were doing,' Theo said.

'I was lucky you were here too. Sorry, to throw you in the deep end. That's the first real emergency I've had to deal with in the six months I've been here.'

*Six months*—that was one question answered.

'What brought you to Byron Bay?'

She shrugged. 'I needed a change of scenery.'

He wanted to ask about Daniel. He wanted to know if he was there too, if Molly was still with him, but there was no subtle way to phrase that question so he let it lie. Her bare ring finger was no clue. Lots of doctors didn't wear rings for practical reasons. It was easier to keep your hands clean if you didn't wear jewellery.

Molly finished her water, stood up and began to tidy the room. She threw out the used sticky pads and packed the defibrillator away after checking that there were more pads in the kit. 'Would you mind putting this back for me?' she asked as she held out the kit, back to avoiding eye contact. 'It goes on the wall outside Paula's office.'

Theo took the kit and left the room, unasked questions still swirling in his brain. But he'd been dismissed. Sent away by Molly. No longer needed.

He returned the kit before heading to the consulting room that had been allocated to him. He ran the cold water in the basin and rinsed his hands to cool them down. He stared into the mirror as he let the water run into the sink, looking at his reflection and wondering if Molly had seen the changes he saw in himself.

He knew he had grown as a person over the past four years but would anyone else notice? Would Molly? Did it matter?

Theo had grown up caught between two cultures, on the outside looking in at kids like Molly and her friends, kids who were comfortable in their skin, who knew where they belonged. He'd never felt completely at ease. He'd often felt he was drifting lonelily between his Asian heritage and his Aussie upbringing. Fitting in nowhere.

His mother was Taiwanese. She'd moved to Australia as a teenager and had met his Australian father at medical school. But although his parents came from different backgrounds their goals were almost identical. Their level of contentment was directly proportional to their level of success—they aspired to successful careers and to raising successful children. But there was some irony there, Theo knew, given that his maternal grandparents had emigrated from Taiwan to look after his sister and him while their parents established their careers and then grew their businesses, having little to do with raising their own children.

Theo was bilingual. Speaking Mandarin with

his grandparents, he'd worked hard to cultivate an Australian accent so that he'd fitted in at school, but he'd known there were more differences between him and his classmates than just an accent. He and his sister were officially Chin Williamses, but Theo had refused to use Chin on his paperwork, preferring to stick with the more Anglicised Williams. Even that hadn't seemed to help. He hadn't eaten the same lunches, he hadn't played sport, his parents and grandparents had never attended assembly or the Christmas concerts and had only occasionally made it to a music recital. He'd given up wishing for attention beyond what he'd garnered by his results. If anything, he knew that was partly what had motivated him to do well at school—it was the only time he'd got any recognition. Any positive attention.

A stint working overseas after graduation had taught him a lot about himself and the world. He had returned knowing the importance of his skills and the importance of human relationships and as he'd settled into his career as a doctor he'd found an identity that had started to fit him. It didn't matter what grades he'd got at school or university once he had his degree. It didn't matter if he played sport, had gone to parties or out on dates. All that mattered was whether he could help his patients. And he had no difficulty with that.

Seeing Molly had thrown him momentarily. He had never expected to run into her here. He'd had no idea she worked for Pacific Coast Clinics. The company was owned by Theo's parents but managed by his mother, a general practitioner, while his father concentrated on his career as a plastic surgeon. They had added the Byron Bay clinic to their stable eighteen months ago but Theo had never given the practice on the upper New South Wales coast much consideration. His time was consumed by his job in Sydney and by his parents' expectations. He was always expected to work harder and longer than the other employees, to prove his value, his skills and his suitability as heir apparent.

He knew he was expected to take over the clinics one day, and he wanted that. But he also knew it wouldn't be handed to him on a plate. He was expected to work for it, and work hard. His parents could just as easily look for an outside investor or one of the other staff members to take over as they could hand him the reins. But they wouldn't be happy. Failure was not an option for a Chin Williams.

When other children had been playing sport and joining teams he'd been doing extra homework or attending tutoring. Not that he'd found schoolwork difficult, but his parents had wanted him and his sister to excel in everything. To be the best. When he was a teenager and schoolmates had been going to parties he'd been at home doing practice exams. His only hobby was playing the guitar and that had developed from the piano lessons he'd been made to take as a child. As a teenager he'd taught himself the guitar and he had entertained fantasies of playing in a band until that dream had been squashed by the demands of university.

His parents and his maternal grandparents had told him, repeatedly, 'You'll never get anywhere without hard work,' and he had to admit, they had a point. He was good at his job and was working hard to establish himself, working harder than the next doctor, trying not only to meet his parents' expectations but to prove to everyone else that he wasn't getting by on his connections.

Personal relationships were another story. He'd had one serious relationship since finishing university, but she had wanted more of his time than he'd had to give. He was only twenty-nine. He figured there was still plenty of time for relationships in his future.

Now, thinking about relationships led him

back to thinking about Molly. He was curious to know what her life had looked like for the past four years. But curiosity was dangerous. It was distracting. Besides, did it really matter? He'd be gone in six weeks and Molly would be firmly back in his past. He needed to stop thinking about her and remember why he was here.

His mother had put her faith in him, her trust, and Theo knew that wasn't easy to come by. He had a job to do in Byron Bay—two jobs: one as a doctor and the other to evaluate the clinic. Its profits had been falling and he had six weeks to figure out why. Normally his mother would have looked into this herself. She'd told him as much. She'd looked over the books but she wanted to see how the clinic functioned in person, but an upcoming overseas conference where she was a keynote speaker had made that impossible so she'd sent Theo in her place. Killing two birds with one stone. He would fill the locum position and get her some answers. Failure was not an option.

Finding out he'd be working with Molly Prescott was a surprise but he wouldn't let it be a complication. They had worked well together today but they weren't friends. They had never been friends and there was no reason to think things would be any different now.

Yes, he'd had a major crush on Molly at university. Yes, he had admired her from a distance. She always seemed so sure of herself and her place in the world and he'd been a little envious of her confidence back then. She was pretty and positive and popular, but there had been one night when he'd found out that she was vulnerable just like anyone else.

He could only remember seeing her let her guard down that once, and it had stayed with him. Not just because of her vulnerability, but because of what else had happened.

He knew the kiss Molly had bestowed on him had been spontaneous, he knew he'd just happened to be the man in front of her when she'd needed comfort, but that hadn't stopped him from kissing her back. And he couldn't pretend the kiss hadn't been incredible. And for a fleeting moment he'd imagined it could be something more than what it was. But just because he wished it didn't make it true.

She'd chosen to kiss him that night, but he knew she wouldn't choose him again permanently. She'd made that much clear. And so he'd walked away.

It had hurt at the time. He had always had Molly on a pedestal, wanting her to notice him, and for a brief moment in time she had.

None of that mattered now. The past was the past. Four years later they were equals. Colleagues. What Molly thought of him now shouldn't matter. He didn't usually care what people thought of him. He was used to existing in his own world. He expected to be judged on his achievements, not for who he was. Molly had been the exception; he had wanted her to see him. For her to see Theo. For some inexplicable reason Molly Prescott had been the only exception in his world.

But as much as he'd like Molly to see the new, confident Theo, she couldn't be an exception again. He wasn't going down that path. He wasn't going to bring up the past. They weren't friends. They were temporary colleagues.

He'd do his job and be gone in six weeks, putting Molly Prescott behind him for the second time. He'd be in and out of Byron Bay before she even had time to notice.

Molly sat down as Theo left her room. She wondered if he'd noticed that she'd almost pushed him out of the door, but she needed a moment to catch her breath alone. All thoughts of tidying up were forgotten as she sat and gathered herself together. She closed her eyes and took a deep breath. Her hands were shaking and she clenched her fists to control the tremor. She knew it wasn't just Warwick's medical episode that had got the adrenalin racing around her body. It was Theo.

All it had taken was a look, one smile, the briefest contact, and she was catapulted right back to the night of their kiss. Everything she'd tried to ignore, how he'd listened, how he'd smelt as he'd held her while she'd cried, how he'd made her feel when he'd given her his attention and how he'd tasted when she'd kissed him, all came rushing back. She liked to pretend she'd forgotten but she knew that was a lie. And now he was here she knew she'd been kidding herself if she'd thought she could pretend it was all in the past.

Molly stared into space as she thought about that night.

She'd had a few drinks, everyone had, but she'd mostly been exhausted and emotional after their final exams. And when she'd seen Daniel in a suspicious embrace with another girl she'd completely lost her temper. It wasn't the first time she'd caught him cheating on her, and she'd been furious. She'd confronted him and they'd gone into the garden and had a massive argument. He'd denied any wrongdoing, she'd been positive he was lying, and he'd left her alone and gone back to the party.

Theo had found her sobbing and he'd sat with

her while she'd blubbered all over him. She hadn't been so drunk that she didn't remember every little detail of their encounter. She'd talked and cried and he'd listened. And then they'd talked to each other. For hours, it had felt like. Molly couldn't remember anyone talking to her for that long. Couldn't recall anyone taking what she said seriously. She was so used to being the life of the party. Being fun. Hiding her insecurities behind a smile and a laugh. But Theo had been interested in what she had to say. And gradually she'd started to feel better. She remembered leaning on his shoulder and then she'd looked up and he'd been watching her with his dark eyes and she'd known he was really seeing her. And then she'd kissed him.

She hadn't asked, she'd just done it, and he'd kissed her back.

She remembered everything. From what they'd talked about to the kiss. Especially the kiss. It had been amazing. Incredible. As if he'd known her for ever, as if he were another half of her. They'd been so in tune, as if they'd kissed a thousand times before, in a thousand different lifetimes. There had been no awkward clashing of teeth or noses. No hesitation.

She'd never been kissed like that.

And then he'd walked away.

And in the months that had followed she'd wondered if she should have grabbed his hand as he'd walked away. If she should have made a different choice. But she'd made the same mistake she'd always made and had forgiven Daniel. And had let Theo go.

She'd been insecure, meticulously curating an image of a girl content with her life, and she'd always been so careful not to let her guard down. Theo had seen her at a weak moment. He had seen and heard too much. She'd never told anyone what happened and she had never spoken to Theo again. She'd moved on with her life, moved on with Daniel and pretended that night had never existed.

She was a different person now. She was finding her independence and didn't need reminders of the past. The spontaneous late-night kiss they'd shared would have to stay consigned to history. And history shouldn't be repeated. Some things needed to be let go. Several years and many reincarnations of her relationship with Daniel had come and gone before she'd finally learned the value of leaving things behind and divesting herself of bad mistakes. It was a lesson she'd do well to remember.

# CHAPTER THREE

AFTER THE RATHER dramatic start, the rest of Theo's first day went smoothly. A couple of billing enquiries had come up that he'd discussed with Paula, leaving him feeling as if he was already making headway with his mother's task. He saw a few patients of Tom's, easing himself into the locum role, before heading to the pub for something to eat.

He sat at the bar nursing a pre-dinner beer. He'd have to find time to get to the supermarket tomorrow. He couldn't eat out every night and he didn't want to eat out alone.

'Hey, Theo.' He was jolted out of his musings by the sound of his name. Matt, one of the physios from the clinic, was standing beside him. He nodded in the direction of Theo's drink as he ordered a beer for himself. 'Can I get you another one?'

'Sure, thanks.'

'I heard you had an eventful first day.'

Theo laughed. 'Yeah. Luckily it turned out okay, but I'm hoping it's not always like that.'

'It's usually pretty chilled here in Byron. This place is all about a good work-life balance.'

'Work-life balance.' Theo laughed. 'I'm not sure what that means.'

'Well, let's hope you have time to find out while you're here. Six weeks, right?'

Theo nodded.

'Have you been to Byron before?'

'Never. Born and bred in Sydney but never been here.'

'You went through med school in Sydney with Molly?'

'Yes. Did she tell you that?' Theo was surprised. He'd got the impression Molly hadn't shared their history.

Matt shook his head as he paid for their beers. 'Gemma did.'

That still meant Molly had told someone. 'I didn't know Molly was in Byron Bay.' He hadn't seen Molly since their graduation ceremony. When it was obvious she and Daniel had patched up their differences. She'd avoided him. He'd left her alone.

He'd felt both disappointed and vindicated when he'd seen them together at graduation. He'd guessed correctly that she would take Daniel back after the party and he hadn't wanted to get caught in the middle of their on-again-off-again romance. He didn't need the headache. As much as he'd been attracted to Molly, and he could admit that he was, he didn't want to be a pawn in her game, cast aside when she went back to Daniel, as she'd done several times throughout university. Being rejected was a form of failure in Theo's eyes and failure was unacceptable, therefore, the sensible thing to do was to reduce his exposure to that risk by removing himself from the situation.

But now he thought again about her bare finger, the lack of a ring, engagement or wedding, and wondered if she was still with Daniel or if she'd come to her senses over the past four years. He hoped for her sake that she had.

'I managed to convince her to make the move up here after she broke up with Daniel,' Matt said.

Theo bit back a smile. Hearing that Molly had broken up with Daniel was good news, but he wondered if it would be like all the other times she'd broken up with him. Was it going to be short-lived or was this it? 'They were still together?' He knew he was fishing for information but he was curious to know what had happened and he took some small measure of satisfaction in hearing Molly and Daniel were no longer a couple.

'Yeah, they were. It's been almost a year since they broke up this time so I'm hoping she's finally done with him. He's not a mate of yours, is he?' Matt added, as if suddenly realising he might be stepping on toes. 'He would have been at university with you too.'

Theo nodded. 'He was in our year but we weren't mates.' Theo and Daniel couldn't have been more different. Theo's parents had worked hard, built a successful business, but they had started with nothing. Theo didn't know Daniel well, but Daniel had clearly been born with a silver spoon in his mouth. He had the arrogance and general disdain of others less fortunate. He had a strong sense of self-importance, an expectation that people would listen to him—not because he had good ideas but because he had grown up having people tell him that he was special. He wasn't Theo's type of person. Theo had never been told he was special. He'd been brought up to work hard, to let his achievements speak for him, but that meant he didn't dare to fail because if he wasn't achieving, then who was he?

He did wonder, though, what it was that had finally made Molly see the light and break up with Daniel. Or had he broken up with her? At university it had always been something that Daniel did that had triggered their breakups. But Molly had taken him back time and time again.

But he wasn't going to ask Matt those questions. It really wasn't any of his business. Molly wasn't his friend; she was just a part of his past. That was where she needed to stay.

Fortunately, Matt had moved on from the topic of Molly. 'What's your trivia knowledge like?' he asked. 'We've got a regular team together for the weekly pub quiz if you'd like to join us. We're down a player—it's usually Tom.'

Theo hesitated. He wasn't sure how Molly would feel if he joined the group. He'd got the impression she wasn't that thrilled to see him.

'No pressure, we're not playing for sheep stations,' Matt said when Theo didn't reply straight away. 'And in the interests of full disclosure, we don't expect to win. We order pizzas and have a few drinks, that's it.'

Theo was assuming Molly would be there. She might not. He made a decision. 'As long as you don't expect me to answer any sports questions,' he replied.

'That's my area of expertise.'

A contest where there were no expectations on him to excel? To be the best? To win? That was a novelty for Theo and one that had some appeal. Perhaps it was time to embrace that work-life balance Matt spoke of. 'Okay, then, sounds good.' He picked up his fresh beer and followed Matt to a table at the back of the pub. It wasn't as if he had anything better to do.

He went round the table, introducing himself to some unfamiliar faces, and as he sat down he saw Molly and Gemma arrive. Her double take when she saw him at the table didn't go unnoticed by him. She looked at the seats around the table. She and Gemma were last to arrive. There was one spare seat on the bench beside Theo and another at the other end of the table. He could tell Molly intended to sit at the far end but Gemma got there first, leaving Molly to sit with him.

Her hip bumped against his as she sat down and immediately she shifted away from him. Could she not bear to be close to him? He moved aside slightly, trying to give her more space. He didn't want her to feel crowded. She looked a little skittish, as though if he said or did the wrong thing she'd get up and leave. Flee. She gave him a smile, but it wasn't her usual full-blown, all-encompassing smile that he remembered. He could see the tension in her shoulders, in her eyes.

She chatted to Matt's partner, Levi, who was a schoolteacher, and then took charge of the answer sheet. Theo suspected that was so she could avoid having to talk to him. That was okay. He didn't need her attention. He wasn't twenty-five any more. He was comfortable in his own skin now, successful, mature. He didn't need to be in awe of Molly any more. Didn't need to be seen by Molly.

Molly knew she'd given Theo short shrift when she'd sat down. She would have preferred to sit somewhere else. She was still on edge.

Working so closely with Theo had reawakened her memory of the kiss. It had been unexpected and amazing. The way it made her feel had surprised her back then, but she'd attributed that to her heightened emotional state and the alcohol. But that didn't explain why she'd had a similar reaction today when Theo had smiled at her and when her arm had brushed against his. He triggered feelings that startled her. Feelings that were out of her control. She didn't like that. She wanted to maintain control.

She was afraid to look at him. Afraid he'd see what she was feeling in her eyes. It really wasn't appropriate and she'd needed time to gather herself together, worried that if she sat beside him he'd know what she was thinking.

So when she'd been forced to take the spot

next to him, she took it upon herself to be the scribe for the group. It gave her an excuse to avoid eye contact but just because she wasn't looking at Theo didn't mean she wasn't aware of his every movement, his every breath. He reached for his drink and his arm brushed hers and the pen skittered over the paper as her skin burned in response to his touch. She tried to focus on the others in the group as the questions began.

Levi had politics and Australian history covered, Gemma was a geography nerd and Matt was all over the sports questions. She was normally good at the trivia questions but her focus was terrible and answers she could normally give without even thinking about eluded her, putting them in the bottom third of the results with two rounds to go.

Theo had contributed a few correct answers in the early rounds but everything changed in the music round. He answered every question correctly, even arguing his case successfully with Levi about the original name of a band and insisting Molly use his answer. They scored full marks and closed the gap on the top two teams. He looked so pleased with his efforts that Molly couldn't ignore him any longer. Not when every other member of the team was so excited to be in with a shot of winning.

'Wow. That was impressive,' she said as Matt took the answer sheet up to the scorer's table. 'How do you know so much about music?' The questions had been varied, it wasn't as if they were all focused on one genre, but Theo had been flawless.

'Music was a big part of my family. My mother believes studying a musical instrument helps to develop the brain so my sister and I had no choice but to learn something. I started with the piano but eventually taught myself the guitar and I have always loved listening to all sorts of music. I really wanted to be in a band but my sister is a classical violinist with the symphony orchestra so, as one of only two children, I was expected to follow in my parents' path and study medicine.'

'You didn't want to be a doctor?'

'I wanted to do both. I spent a lot of time at live gigs, soaking up that atmosphere, until it became impossible with the time commitments and hours needed to devote to study. But it's still my way of relaxing.'

'Do you still play the guitar?' Molly asked, realising she knew nothing about him really.

He nodded.

Molly couldn't play an instrument. She could

never sit still for long enough to learn. She played netball, a lot of netball. That was much more her speed.

He had musician's hands, slender fingers, fine bones. But Molly supposed they were good doctor's hands too. Gentle. Tender. She lifted her eyes to his face. He had a shadow of a beard on his chin and jaw, slightly darker where a moustache would grow, and his eyes were almost black in the dim light of the pub.

'Molly, are you ready for the last round?'

Matt's question interrupted Molly's thoughts and she jumped and dragged her gaze away from Theo. She reached for a fresh sheet of paper to record the answers but Theo reached for it at the same time and his fingers landed on hers. A burst of heat shot up her left arm and Molly dropped the paper in a fluster. She tucked her hand under the table, opening and closing her fist until the tingling subsided and normal feeling returned and she was able to rest that hand on the answer sheet to stabilise it as she wrote. Her heart was racing and she could feel a frown of concentration creasing her brow as she struggled to keep focused and keep up with the answers her team was peppering her with. Theo's knee bumped against her thigh as he reached for his drink, disrupting her focus even further, and at the end of the round she got up quickly, needing to put some distance between her and Theo lest she make another silly mistake.

It was impossible to avoid Theo completely though as the next morning, as she was rushing into the clinic, late as usual, he was waiting for her in her consulting room.

He handed her a coffee and a paper bag.

Molly took the coffee and peered inside the bag to find it contained a doughnut. 'What's this for?'

'An apology.'

Molly frowned. 'Apology?'

'I get the impression you would prefer me not to be here.'

'Here?'

'In Byron Bay. Working at the clinic. Coming to the quiz night. Anywhere really.'

Theo's dark eyes were flat as he watched her closely. His eyes lacked their usual shine and made her feel uncomfortable. Had she made him feel unwelcome? That hadn't been her intention.

'Can we call a truce?' he asked, taking her silence for affirmation of his thoughts. 'I don't know why you don't want me here but I'm hoping we can get on as colleagues. I promise I'm not going to bite you. Or kiss you again.'

'You remembered.' Of course he did. But she wasn't sure how she felt about him putting that information out there between them. She was part mortified, part pleased. She didn't want to be forgettable but she would have preferred the incident to be wiped from memory. His memory. She was no longer the insecure girl who was looking for attention and seeking validation and she worried that Theo might still see her as such. Despite her having resolved to overcome the damage that Daniel had done, that her parents had done, she feared her insecurities hadn't been erased completely, and having her past and present collide could destabilise her carefully laid plan of reinvention.

'That kiss was a lot of things but forgettable wasn't one of them,' Theo said, and Molly could feel herself blushing as he continued. 'I promise I'm not here to cause drama. I don't want to make things difficult for you.'

His dark eyes were gleaming again, his gaze gentle, unchallenging, and Molly knew he wasn't looking for an argument, he was offering her a way out. Telling her he had moved past their last encounter so she could put it behind her too.

'I'm only here for forty days. Do you think you can put up with me for that long?'

She nodded, rather unconvincingly she felt,

but she couldn't ignore his question altogether. It wasn't a case of putting up with him. It was a case of maintaining her composure. She knew she'd crossed a line the night she'd kissed him but it had been so nice to have someone ask her if she was okay, to have someone listen to her. She hadn't expected the kiss to tip her world sideways. And for one crazy minute she'd been tempted to take a chance and see what would happen if she chose Theo. But for so long she had been hiding behind a mask. One that Daniel hadn't even cared enough to see behind. She'd been the loudest in the room, the funniest, the brightest and she was terrified that if her mask slipped Theo might not like what he found behind it.

But she still wasn't sure she'd be able to handle being colleagues without being awkward. She got the feeling Theo could read her innermost thoughts. That he could see into her heart and soul, and she didn't want him to read her thoughts now. She didn't want him to know she'd never forgotten him or the kiss either. Those days were long gone.

Theo was the last one in the clinic on Friday night. He had spoken to his mother and run through the issues he'd already identified within the clinic and then returned to the spreadsheets when the call ended, but the figures were swimming in circles.

He kept thinking about Molly and wondering why it was that they found themselves together in this town. Was it fate, as his mother and grandparents would attest to, or was it simply a coincidence, as his father would say? And, either way, did it mean anything?

His logical side told him it didn't, but he still couldn't concentrate. Work could wait for another day, he decided as he shut down his computer.

But now the weekend stretched ahead of him. He had no plans. He never did—he was normally working.

He wondered what Molly was doing. But if she had plans she hadn't included him, not that he expected her to, and nor had he asked her what she was up to.

He had to admit he still felt a pull of attraction, chemistry, a buzz when he was around her. She still bewitched him, that hadn't changed. But he wasn't going to make a move. He was only here for another month or so and it was almost as if they'd agreed to ignore one another for that time. Despite their truce, they'd barely said a word to each other for the past two days.

He switched off the lights and locked the clinic behind him. He walked through town, heading for the beach and home. Town was busy and loud but he assumed it was par for the course on a Friday night before remembering that the Schoolies Festival started this weekend. Hadn't Tom said the festival organisers were looking for volunteers? Perhaps he should look into that. It might fill up his time. He couldn't spend all weekend looking at spreadsheets.

Work-life balance. That was what he needed. He wasn't sure if spending his weekend volunteering in the first-aid tent counted as finding work-life balance but he didn't really know any other way to live. He'd been brought up to work hard, study hard, commit one hundred per cent to his endeavours and reach his goals. He understood the work bit but what about the life bit?

Time off was rare and he usually spent it in the gym—not because he loved it but because he knew the benefits—and to relax he turned to his music.

He unlocked his front door, picked up his guitar from the lounge, grabbed a beer from the fridge and headed out to the deck that overlooked the beach. He finished his beer and then played some chords as he looked over the ocean. He let his mind empty as the notes floated around him, accompanied by the intermittent blink of the lighthouse to his right and the stars overhead.

* * *

Molly pulled on a pair of jeans and the green T-shirt she'd been given to wear as her uniform for tonight. She and Gemma had done their regular Saturday morning walk up to the lighthouse followed by a swim, but had forgone their usual time on the beach as the sand was already being overrun by the school leavers who had arrived in town for the Schoolies Festival, which officially started today. Molly had spent the afternoon cleaning and doing the grocery shopping before she headed to the foreshore, where she would volunteer her time in the first-aid tent for the first night of the festival.

Having volunteered last year, she thought she was prepared for anything but what she wasn't ready for was seeing Theo, also wearing the green volunteers' T-shirt, walking into the tent in front of her.

'Theo! What are you doing here?'

'Volunteering.'

Molly frowned. 'Why?' Their little contact this past week had meant she was beginning to think she could navigate working with him, treating him as just a doctor she had been to university with, as a nine-to-five weekday colleague, but she hadn't counted on spending Saturday night with him as well.

'Tom said they were short of volunteers and I figured I didn't have anything better to do this weekend.'

Molly immediately felt guilty. Hadn't anyone from the clinic offered to show him around? What had happened to small-town hospitality? 'You didn't check out the beaches or the town?'

'I thought I'd avoid the beaches until after the festival—I'm not sure I wanted to share it with a thousand school leavers. I did take a drive up into the Hinterland but that still left me with a Saturday night to fill.'

Perhaps she should have sent him off with Matt. That would have meant she could avoid the situation she now found herself in, namely spending the next few hours together, she thought as they were greeted by Steph, one of the volunteer coordinators.

Steph introduced Theo and Molly to the other volunteers—Justin and Priya, both first aiders—before showing them around the large tent, which was actually several marquees joined together to create different spaces. The front section of the tent was set up as a dispensary where first aiders could hand out water, sunburn cream, painkillers and lollies to the festival-goers. A cluster of beanbags had been arranged in one corner of the tent to give kids a break-out space if they needed a chance to chill, and a couple of smaller tents at the back had been furnished with beds where treatment for minor injuries or ailments could be administered away from the crowds.

'It's fantastic to have you both here tonight,' Steph said as they returned to the front of the tent. 'We are grateful to have as many volunteers as we can get but always happy to have some with more medical experience. We've got some nurses and paramedics helping throughout the week too. Your expertise won't always be needed but occasionally we can have more serious injuries and, because the hospital is a ten-minute drive out of town, it's not easy for the kids to present to emergency, and we don't really want them turning up there as the first option for every little mishap. The first-aid tent helps to triage the load.'

'If we do need to send someone to hospital, how do we manage that?' Theo asked.

'We can call an ambulance in an emergency or, if it's not critical, someone from the Red Frogs brigade can take them.'

'The Red what?'

'Red Frogs are another volunteer group,' Steph explained. 'They're affiliated with a church group so they're separate from the first-aid crew, not all of them have first-aid skills, and they provide general support, emotional support, advice and information. For a lot of these kids this week will be the first time they've been away from home without some sort of adult supervision. Some of them get in over their heads and need support, others can find the whole experience a bit overwhelming. The Red Frogs act kind of like a big brother. Or sister. Support without judgement. They will drift in and out of our tent over the course of the night but they're around all week for the students. The kids can download an app that lets them contact Red Frogs for assistance or company, and they've been known to offer everything from pancake cook-ups, room visits and cleans to emotional support, walking kids home and handing out lolly frogs,' she said as she pointed to a huge bowl filled with red frog-shaped lollies that sat on one of the counters. 'Theo, why don't you take a few minutes to familiarise yourself with the treatment spaces before it gets busy? Molly can show you the ropes.'

'You've done this before?' Theo asked as Steph left them to it.

Molly nodded and headed for the treatment area, knowing it was easier to talk to Theo if she wasn't looking at him at the same time. That way she could avoid the fluttery feeling she got every time she looked into his eyes. 'I volunteered last year,' she said. 'I came up for a holiday and one week of my trip just happened to coincide with the Schoolies Festival. Matt and Levi volunteer with the Red Frogs and Matt talked me into helping out. I really enjoyed it.'

That wasn't the whole truth. Matt had invited her for a holiday when she'd broken up with Daniel and, to keep her occupied while he was at work, Matt had suggested she lend a hand during the festival. She had enjoyed it and it had kept her mind busy, given her an excuse to avoid Daniel's phone calls and given her a chance to experience life in Byron. 'I felt like I really got to know some of the locals and it was a big part of helping me to make the decision to relocate here permanently.'

'What presentations were you dealing with?' Theo asked.

'Sunburn and dehydration during the day, drug- and alcohol-affected kids later on, plus the odd broken bone and a concussion or two, but be prepared for anything,' she said. 'The first night was pretty hectic last year. The kids tend to party hard over the first weekend and then calm down as the week progresses and the excitement wears off. Once the exhaustion and hangovers kick in, they can't continue on at the same pace.'

The end of Molly's sentence was drowned out by loud cheering and yelling coming from the beach. The first-aid tent had been erected on the grassy plateau overlooking the beach, between the surf club and the pub on the corner, and the noise from the sand competed with the sound of music from the hotel. Drawn by the commotion, Theo and Molly wandered back to the front of the tent.

Sunset was approaching and the Norfolk pines cast long shadows on the lawn where several teenagers sat, feasting on takeaway. Main Beach stretched out in front of them, full of school leavers. The foreshore was an alcohol-free zone. Those who were old enough could drink at the pub, but, judging by the volume of noise and some of the rowdy behaviour, it looked as though plenty of those on the beach had made their way there from the bar. Behind them the pub was also busy, music blared from the speakers and Molly knew there would be a live band later in the night.

Her attention was drawn back to the beach where the sounds of cheering were being accompanied by rhythmic clapping. From their slightly elevated vantage point she could see a large group of kids on the sand forming a circle around four others. The circle gave the tableau the effect of a bullring. Within the circle were two boys, each with a girl sitting on top of his shoulders.

'What are they doing?' Theo asked.

The two girls each held what appeared to be long sticks but Molly knew they were actually beer cans that had been taped together.

'Playing beer-can jousting,' she said.

As the crowd cheered and clapped the two boys ran towards each other, the girls bouncing on their shoulders. The girls had the beer-can sticks thrust out in front of them, aiming at their opposition number. Molly heard Theo's sharp intake of breath as the stick of one girl glanced off the other girl's shoulder, causing her to overbalance. She tumbled into the sand as the crowd clapped and whistled. Molly held her breath until the girl got to her feet and bowed to the crowd as the other girl held her arms aloft in a victory pose.

The boys retreated to opposite sides of the circle and a new girl took the place of the one who had fallen. She waited for someone to hand her the jousting stick before the boys ran at each other again.

'Shouldn't we stop them? Someone is going to get hurt.'

Molly was watching through half-closed eyes, as if that were going to make the activity safer, but as the words left Theo's mouth she saw one girl rear backwards as the jousting stick hit her in the face. As she fell, she took all the other combatants down with her and suddenly there was a pile of bodies in the centre of the circle. The crowd, which seconds before had been loud and boisterous, fell silent.

# CHAPTER FOUR

WITHOUT DISCUSSION MOLLY and Theo sprinted to the beach.

Theo pushed his way through to the middle of the crowd and Molly followed closely behind him, letting him clear a path for her. All four kids were kneeling in the sand as Theo and Molly squatted beside them. The boys appeared to have got out of the contest unscathed but the same could not be said for the girls. One had a nasty gash above her eye, which was bleeding profusely, and the other girl was clutching her mouth as blood streamed down her chin.

'Let me see.' Molly didn't bother introducing herself. Her green T-shirt identified her as a first aider and her tone implied authority. The girl took her hand away from her mouth and Molly could see a gap where a front tooth should be.

Molly looked up and saw Justin, one of the other volunteers. 'We're looking for a lost tooth,' she said, assuming the girl had started the day with both her front teeth. Looking for the tooth would be like trying to find a needle in a haystack, but it would keep everyone busy while she and Theo sorted out the injured girls.

She helped her patient to her feet while looking around for Theo. He was still squatting in the sand next to his patient. He'd ripped off his T-shirt and had it pressed against her head wound, stemming the blood. His skin was smooth and golden and his shoulder muscles flexed as he reached for the girl's elbow to help her stand. With difficulty Molly dragged her gaze away from Theo's bare back and naked chest. It was a struggle. It was a reflex reaction to let her eyes roam over his body, but she couldn't afford to get distracted.

'If you find the tooth, give it to Justin. Try not to touch the root of the tooth.' Molly issued instructions to the crowd. 'Justin, I'll send someone down with a container. If by some miracle it is found, bring it up to the tent as quickly as you can.'

She and Theo helped the girls up to the first-aid tent while dozens of kids dropped to their hands and knees and began sifting through the sand.

Molly and Theo sat the girls on adjacent treatment beds, not bothering to pull across the curtains that separated them. She pulled on a pair of surgical gloves and opened a container of saline, pouring some into a small specimen jar and handing it to Priya, the other volunteer. 'Take this down to Justin,' she said. 'If they find the tooth, get Justin to put it in there and bring it back to me.'

Priya raised her eyebrows. 'You think they'll find it?'

Molly shrugged. 'Stranger things have happened.' She had no way of knowing if they'd have any luck but they had to try.

She poured some saline into a cup and handed it to her patient. 'Rinse your mouth and spit into here,' she said as she held a stainless-steel bowl out for her. She handed the bowl to Steph, who was hovering nearby, to empty. 'Is there an after-hours dentist on standby this week?' she asked Steph.

Steph nodded as she rinsed the bowl.

'Can you give them a call and see if they'll meet us at the surgery?' Molly asked as she tore open a packet of gauze and held it to the girl's gum to soak up the blood and stem the bleeding. All the blood was coming from the gum. Her lip was intact so she wouldn't require stitches. Hopefully the tooth would be found but, either way, she needed a dental review.

Molly glanced over to Theo as Steph left the area and Priya returned, without the missing tooth. Theo put her to work helping him cut sutures as he stitched the girl's head wound. He was still shirtless, Steph would need to find him a new top, but Molly secretly hoped she wasn't in too much of a hurry. She admired Theo's physique while she admired his handiwork. His stitches were small and neat and Molly doubted anyone would be able to tell that a plastic surgeon hadn't done the job. He was applying a dressing over the stitches when Justin appeared, triumphantly holding the jar of saline, complete with the missing tooth.

'You found it!'

Justin nodded and handed the jar over to Molly. She opened the lid, put the jar on the bed and changed her gloves. She opened a fresh packet of gauze before removing the blood-soaked wadding from her patient's mouth. She carefully removed the tooth from the jar and pushed it back into the socket.

'Bite down gently on the gauze,' she told her patient as she placed the fresh wad under the repositioned tooth. 'It'll hold the tooth in place until we get you to the dentist.' Molly turned to Justin. 'Can we get one of the Red Frogs to do the transfer to the dental surgery?'

Justin nodded and he and Priya took Molly's patient, leaving Molly alone with Theo and the second girl. He was doing a concussion test before he checked on any allergies and gave her some tablets for pain relief. Once he was finished and had given her the all-clear, Molly grabbed another Red Frog to take the girl back to her accommodation to rest. Priya, Steph and Justin all drifted back to the front of the tent and suddenly it was just the two of them again.

Molly pulled off her gloves and threw them in the bin before sanitising her hands. Theo did the same and then picked up the spare T-shirt Steph had left for him and pulled it over his head. Molly tried not to be disappointed. Wasn't this exactly what she'd been trying to avoid? Letting herself get too close to Theo, letting him get too close to her. And this definitely counted as too close.

'What a stupid game that is,' Theo said as he tugged the T-shirt down over his stomach. 'They're lucky someone didn't lose an eye.'

Molly smiled. Theo was so incensed. She knew it wasn't funny but it was hard not to find his reaction a little amusing. 'Anyone one would think you were seventy-nine, not twenty-nine,' she said. 'Didn't you ever do anything stupid when you were younger?'

'No, never,' Theo replied, but he was grinning and Molly wasn't sure if he was pulling her leg or not.

'Did you go to Schoolies Week?' she asked.

Theo shook his head. 'My parents took my sister and me overseas when I finished school. I think it was their way of making sure I didn't get into any trouble. My parents both had high expectations. My sister and I didn't get a lot of freedom. It wasn't until I went to university that I really had a chance to test the waters and you'd think spending time at music gigs I'd push a few boundaries, but I was always conscious of my grades. I couldn't afford to let things slip. Failure wasn't an option in our house so I never really went wild. You?'

'Did I go wild or did I go to Schoolies?'

'Both.'

'I did go to Schoolies. And lived to tell the tale, obviously.'

'Did you have fun?'

'Definitely.' She smiled. 'It was the first time I'd been away with my friends without any parents. We had an absolute blast. But if it makes you feel any better, the police will crack down on the kids a bit later in the night. Apparently on the first night they like to take a couple of kids off to the police station on some trumped-up charges, urinating in public, underage drinking, that sort of thing, which serves to scare the majority of the kids into behaving a little better. There will still be some who want to push the boundaries but most of them don't want to get sent home or spend the night in a cell. They've paid a lot of money to spend a week here—forking out for accommodation, entertainment, meals, drinks—and they don't want to miss out on the fun, so things will calm down.'

As if to back up her point the next couple of hours were relatively quiet. Molly had to extract a nasty splinter from a boy's hand and Theo sent another to hospital for an X-ray on a suspected broken toe, and then it was mostly handing out bottles of water and vomit bags before sending kids home under the supervision of the Red Frogs.

'I'm starving,' Theo said when their shift ended at midnight. 'Is there anywhere we can grab a feed this late?'

'The pub will be open,' Molly told him. 'And they provide volunteers with a free cheeseburger and fries, or a tofu burger if that's your preference. It is Byron Bay, after all.'

'Sounds good. Would you like to join me?'

'Sure.' She justified the extra time with Theo by telling herself she was hungry so it made sense to grab some food. And it would ease her guilty conscience that no one had thought to play host and had left Theo to his own devices on his first weekend. But really, she had enjoyed his company tonight.

'That was an interesting night,' Theo said as they waited for their burgers. 'I must say I didn't expect to find myself tending to exuberant teenagers in a tent on the beach at midnight as part of my time here.'

'No, it's a bit left of centre, isn't it?' Molly laughed. 'It suits Byron Bay though.'

'I didn't expect to find you here either. I always imagined you married to Daniel and living in Sydney.'

His comment surprised her. His assumptions were probably reasonable enough, but she was surprised to hear he'd thought about her at all. 'And yet, here I am,' she said, 'neither of those things.'

'Here you are,' he agreed. He was looking at her intently and Molly could feel her heart beating in her chest as she stood in the spotlight of Theo's attention. His dark eyes held her in their thrall as she held her breath, waiting for some sort of personal declaration she felt was coming.

'Order for Molly!'

She jumped, startled out of her reverie by the

everyday sound of her name being called, and the moment was lost. Theo glanced over his shoulder and their connection was broken as he went to collect their burgers.

'Do you want to eat here?' he asked as he handed her order to her.

Molly shook her head. The pub was still busy and noisy, filled with school leavers intent on celebrating into the wee hours of the morning, and she needed some peace and quiet, some time to sort out the thoughts in her head. 'I've had enough of exuberant teenagers tonight,' she said, copying Theo's earlier description. 'I'll have mine to go.'

'Are you walking home?'

'I should be but I drove into town. I was running late.' She smiled and Theo laughed.

'Again.'

'Again,' she said. 'I parked at the clinic.'

'I'll walk with you to your car.'

Molly was about to say she'd be fine, it was only a short walk, but she realised she wasn't quite ready to say goodnight to Theo. She didn't want to admit that seeing him half undressed might have had something to do with that. But regardless of his state of dress they'd worked well together tonight and she was feeling much more comfortable with him.

'Okay, thanks.' She ate a couple of fries as they walked and then picked up the previous thread of conversation. 'Why did you assume I'd be married to Daniel?' she asked. She was intrigued to know if he'd spent a lot of time thinking about her, but of course she couldn't ask him that.

'You seemed so serious about him, so convinced he was the right man for you. I thought you might have married him. But I was pleased to find out you haven't.'

'You never liked him,' Molly stated. She knew that. Theo had made that clear.

'I didn't dislike him. I didn't like him for you. I thought you could do better.'

Molly smiled. She wasn't offended by Theo's view. She agreed with him now. 'You were right,' she said. 'But I needed to figure that out for myself. It turns out I'm not a very fast learner when it comes relationships, but I had no intention of getting married.'

'To Daniel?'

'To anyone.'

'Really? Not ever?'

'Marriage seems like a strange commitment to make. To be bound to someone until the end of time. I think it just opens you up to heartache and I haven't seen anything yet to make me change my mind. I'm focusing on myself and on my career. Taking some time out for self-reflection.'

'And what are you discovering? I assume you're not about to swap life as a doctor to move to the hinterland and grow herbs?'

'Only medicinal ones,' she teased.

'A worthy pastime, I agree,' he said with a smile that made his eyes gleam and her heart skip a beat, 'but that seems a waste of a medical degree. Or is medicine not a calling for you?'

Molly looked at Theo as she wondered how much she should admit. 'To be honest, becoming a doctor wasn't my idea. The careers advisor at school suggested it as an option. She thought I'd get the grades and I thought if I got into med school it might make my dad notice me. I am the middle of three girls and I always thought Dad was disappointed that he didn't have any sons. He never had a lot of time for us—he was the headmaster at a boys' school and he spent a lot of time at work—and I thought if I became a doctor I might suddenly become worthy of his attention. The school he taught at was very academic and there was the expectation that almost all of the students would go on to university and to study prestigious courses. Law. Medicine. Engineering. Politics. Medicine was something I could imagine doing.' She shrugged.

'Did it work?'

'Nope.' She threw her empty fries container into a council bin and unwrapped her cheeseburger. 'Turns out it wasn't our gender that was the issue. My father wasn't a faithful husband. I had always assumed he would spend more time with us if we were boys. I never considered that he was not at home because he was cheating on my mother. When I was fifteen, I saw my father with another woman. He told me my mother knew. It turned out she did know and she chose to stay with him anyway. For a long time I believed that was normal behaviour in a marriage and I decided that if that was the case, then I didn't want to get married. Marriage should be about commitment, trust, fidelity and love. I didn't see it being about any of those things.

'And then I met Daniel and he was the same, but I thought I could be the one to get him to change. To commit. I don't know why I didn't look for a faithful partner instead.' She paused, unsure how to continue, not sure if Theo would judge her but needing him to understand who she had been back then. 'Dad was a serial philanderer. He had plenty of opportunity. He is handsome, charming—the mothers of his students couldn't get enough, apparently. What I couldn't understand was why my mother didn't kick him out. So, I asked her that question. She said she didn't know how to survive on her own, or as a single mother, and she was scared of what her future would look like if she left.'

Theo was looking at her and she knew what he was thinking. 'I know. I was doing the same thing with Daniel, taking him back every time he apologised and promised to be better. I'd take him back hoping this time he meant it but knowing it wouldn't last. I was repeating my mother's mistakes but at least I hadn't married him. I knew I could take care of myself financially. That was another big reason why medicine appealed to me—it was a high-income-earning job that would give me financial independence. If I was never getting married, I needed to earn my own money. I never wanted to be dependent on someone else for my financial security. Luckily for me it turned out that I love being a doctor.'

Unlike for her mother, it wasn't financial security that had influenced her decisions and kept her in a relationship with Daniel. Molly had spent most of her life wanting to be seen and she'd been afraid that if she wasn't Daniel's girlfriend any more, if she wasn't part of the cool crowd, then she'd suddenly become invisible again. That fear had been real enough to keep her going back, long after it was good for her.

She kept her eyes focused on the footpath. She hadn't expected to talk about Daniel, hadn't expected to share her thoughts with Theo, but he was a good listener and she felt safe with him. They'd worked well together tonight, and she'd been comfortable in his company while they were busy and, somehow, that feeling continued as they walked side by side in the dark, making it easy to confide in him.

'I kept telling myself I could leave whenever I wanted, but I never did. Not permanently. I'd break up with him and then take him back. Time after time after time. I'd invested so much time and effort into that relationship that it made it hard to throw it away, but I'm done now. I've been here nearly six months and I'm surviving. Better than that, I'm happy here. Away from my family. Away from Daniel. It was the best decision I ever made.'

'What made your mind up?'

'After the last time he cheated on me I realised I was exactly like my mother, just without a wedding ring. Normally the pattern would be he'd cheat on me briefly, give up the other girl and convince me to give him another chance. I suppose I'd always let him get away with his behaviour, I'd condoned it in a way. Once I became aware of the situation with my parents and had seen how my father treated my mother, and how she put up with it, I think I came to believe that it was just the way men were. The way relationships were. The way my relationship was.

'But the last time was different. He wanted me back but wanted to keep seeing the other girl as well. I had just enough self-esteem to reject that sordid offer. I had a career, my own income, no dependants. I didn't need Daniel, but it wasn't until I finally realised that I didn't want him, or the life that he was subjecting me to, any more that I did something about changing things.' She smiled. 'It's ironic really—you told me the same things years ago. But I wasn't ready to hear it then. Matt helped.'

'Have you and Matt been friends for a long time?'

'No, we met playing social netball before he moved up here, but it think it was a case of the planets aligning. He was back in Sydney for a mutual friend's engagement party when Daniel and I were on a break. Another one. Matt convinced me to come up here for a holiday and I loved it. But when I got back to Sydney I realised I needed to make the change and I left for the last time.'

'That was brave.'

Molly shook her head. 'Not really. It was well overdue but I was glad to make Daniel someone else's problem.'

'Is he still with her?'

'I don't know. I try not to think about him if I can help it.'

'Ah.'

Molly frowned. 'What?'

'Is that why you weren't happy to see me? Because I reminded you of Daniel?'

How was it possible that Theo had more insight into Molly than she'd had into herself? 'You didn't remind me of Daniel, but you did remind me of a time in my past I'm not proud of. You reminded me of the person I was then—insecure, dependent, like my mother—all the things I swore I wasn't going to be. I wanted to believe that I was growing as a person, that this move to Byron Bay was the start of a new life, a new me, and your arrival brought back some of my insecurities.

'Until I realised that I couldn't put that onto you. I'm responsible for myself and I know I'm not that person any more. I've made some tough decisions and I've made some good ones and some bad ones, but I'm starting to think the good are outweighing the bad now. Moving here has been a good one. I love the job, my colleagues and the town.'

'I'm pleased. You seem happy.'

'I am. And I've got a chance to figure out who I am now. Who I want to be and who I want to be with. I haven't been on my own since I was seventeen. This is my time to work on myself.'

'Do you think this is a permanent move for you?'

'I'm not sure. But I think it could be.'

'You like it here? You're not missing the rat race of Sydney?'

'Not at all. I love it here. The job is great, the people are lovely. It's fun. What about you? Is Byron Bay casting its spell over you yet? I would have thought the rock star part of you would like the vibe of Byron.'

'You know what, I kind of do. It's a lot more relaxed here, isn't it? I feel like even the drama of tonight will be forgotten by tomorrow. People seem to live in the moment.'

'That's a good way of putting it. I'm not sure that it's sustainable for a lot of people to live like that but it's appealing for a little while. Something to be said for being able to stop and smell the metaphorical roses.'

'Even the clinic seems a little less frenetic. Often I feel like I'd get more job satisfaction if

I could spend more time with my patients but there never seem to be enough hours in the day. But the past few days have been a revelation. I've enjoyed having more time and longer consults.'

'I think that's one nice thing about regional medicine. We get the chance to know our patients a bit better,' Molly said as they reached the car park.

The walk had taken a lot longer than it needed to and Molly realised they'd both been dawdling, so caught up in their conversation there hadn't seemed any need to hurry. Perhaps the slow pace of Byron Bay was to blame or perhaps they had been happy to spend more time in each other's company.

'This is me,' she said as she pushed the button to unlock her car. Theo reached for the door and opened it for her. She stepped into the opening and then spun around to face him. 'Thanks for keeping me company and thanks for listening.' Listening was still one of his strong suits.

'Any time.'

Molly leant her back on the car, reluctant to get in, reluctant to say goodnight. 'Can I give you a lift home?' she offered.

'Which way are you headed?'

'Up the hill.' She gestured to her right. 'Towards the lighthouse.'

Theo shook his head. 'I'm the other way. It's only a short walk.'

He was standing close, on the same side of the door as her. He had one arm resting along the top of the door, keeping it open. If Molly stood up straight, if she leant forwards and moved away from the car, she'd almost be touching him. She closed her hand into a fist and forced herself to keep it by her side, resisting the sudden and ridiculous desire to reach for him.

She maintained her position, frozen in place, too scared to move, knowing if she straightened up as she'd have to do to climb into the car it would bring her closer to him. She was scared of what she might do then.

Theo hadn't moved. He was watching her with his dark eyes and, worried that he might read her thoughts, she dropped her gaze.

But that was a mistake.

Now she was looking at his mouth.

He had an amazing mouth. His lips were full and soft and just begged to be kissed. But that hadn't ended well last time and she didn't want to repeat the same mistake, no matter how tempting. She shouldn't have kissed him four years ago and she shouldn't kiss him again. Not now. She was avoiding relationships, taking time to work on herself, but when Theo was standing in front of her it made her wonder if complete abstinence was a step too far.

But kissing Theo wouldn't serve any purpose other than to satisfy an urge and she'd learnt her lesson. It hadn't been fair of her to kiss him spontaneously four years ago and she wasn't about to do it again. Next time they kissed it would be consensual. Next time she would ask first.

Molly shook her head—what was she thinking? Next time! She was getting carried away in the moment. She needed to ignore the frisson of awareness and the shiver in her belly that she got whenever Theo smiled at her or whenever his hand touched hers or whenever he took off his shirt. It shouldn't be impossible. Even though it felt as if it might be.

Once again Molly tried to keep her distance from Theo over the next few days. The pull of attraction she'd felt had frightened her. She didn't want to get involved. She didn't want to be in a relationship. Relationships complicated life, made her part of something else, someone else, and what she really needed was time alone, time to be by herself, time to figure herself out. She'd been asked out a few times since moving to Byron Bay, but it was easy to turn down those invitations when there'd been no chemistry. But it was becoming hard to ignore the spark of awareness she felt whenever she saw Theo.

The connection she felt was strong, the pull powerful. It shouldn't have surprised her, she'd felt it before, four years ago but that was exactly why she needed to keep her distance. Her brain and her body were at odds with each other. One pushing. One pulling. One resisting. One capitulating. She was worried she'd do something stupid if she spent too much time with Theo.

It was easy enough to avoid him in the mornings because she was always dashing in the door at the last minute, and she cut down on her caffeine intake to avoid bumping into him in the staff kitchen. Thankfully there was no quiz night at the pub this week because of the Schoolies Festival, so by Thursday she thought she might make it through the whole week without seeing him. Until she found herself face to face with him at the hydrotherapy pool.

Thank God he wasn't actually in the pool, but standing beside it, fully clothed, talking to Matt. But still, her stomach flipped and her hands became clammy. If she hadn't been taking a patient through in preparation for their first hydrotherapy session she would have turned on her tail and fled.

She needed to get a grip. She was being ridiculous. She tried reminding herself why she meant to keep her distance from him but when he saw her approaching and smiled at her she couldn't remember a single reason.

She sent her patient to the change rooms and, telling herself it was just the humidity of the indoor pool making her hands clammy, she forced herself to keep walking, one step at a time, towards Matt. And Theo.

Matt was explaining the benefits of hydrotherapy to Theo. 'I'd really like to get into the pool more often, but I just don't have the time between patients,' Matt said. 'We need more staff in order to run more regular sessions.'

'Is the pool used for anything else?' Theo asked as Molly waited for her patient.

'Like what?'

'Kids' swimming lessons? Aquarobics?'

Molly frowned and wondered why Theo was asking all these questions.

'No,' Matt replied.

'So it is underutilised.'

Matt nodded as Molly waved her patient over.

'Matt, this is Susan Ford. She's got her first hydro session today.'

Matt took Susan off and Molly walked out

of the pool area with Theo. 'What's with all the questions?' she asked.

'I was just curious to see how it all works.'

She didn't understand why it mattered. He was only a locum. 'You don't have hydrotherapy in the Sydney clinic?'

'No. We don't have any allied health facilities. This clinic has a different operating structure. I'm just trying to see what works and what doesn't.'

That still didn't explain his interest, but it wasn't really any of her business. Perhaps he was thinking about offering hydrotherapy back at his clinic in Sydney. If he wanted to get to know the intricacies of the clinic, that was his choice. She just needed to worry about getting through one more day until it was the weekend, when she could relax and not have to worry about bumping into him.

Molly grabbed a handful of red lolly frogs from a bowl in the first-aid tent and sat on the edge of a treatment bed, swinging her legs as she popped a lolly into her mouth.

'I thought they were meant for the kids,' Theo teased her.

Molly's heart leapt at his voice and she almost choked on the lolly.

Her hope that he wouldn't also be volunteering on the last official night of the Schoolies Festival was well and truly quashed. There seemed to be no way of avoiding him completely. He was constantly popping up in her vicinity, so much so that she wasn't really all that surprised to see him tonight.

'I don't think they'll miss a few,' she replied. 'This is what keeps me coming back.'

'Not my company?'

'I didn't know you were going to be here.'

'I had a good time last weekend and figured I could lend a hand again. The gig came highly recommended,' he said with a smile.

He had a really lovely smile, Molly thought, not for the first time. She'd miss seeing his smile once he returned to Sydney. She'd miss the way it made her feel. But every time he smiled at her she felt her resistance to spending time with him crumbling just a little bit more until one day she feared she wouldn't have any resolve left. And where would that leave her? Throwing caution to the wind and kissing him again?

She shook her head. She couldn't do that. Perhaps she was experiencing a simple case of sexual frustration? Perhaps she needed to rethink her relationship ban—maybe she needed to go on a date and try casual sex. That might get thoughts of Theo out of her head and let her start a clean slate.

The only problem was she'd never had a one-night stand or casual sex and she didn't know if she could. But that might be her best option, she thought as she put another lolly frog in her mouth and looked for something to do to keep her hands busy and her mind engaged on something other than Theo.

The first few hours of their shift were fairly routine. They handed out plenty of water and treated a boy who'd got into a fight and broken a bone in his hand, but they hadn't been called upon much at all.

The kids were down at the beach where a DJ was playing and the rest of the volunteers were milling around the edges of the rave, handing out bottles of water and keeping an eye on things. Molly and Theo were alone in the tent, waiting for anything more serious that might need their expertise.

Though she'd been on edge initially, she'd gradually relaxed into things. Even though she sometimes felt as if Theo could read her mind, she knew that wasn't really the case. He didn't know that she'd wanted to kiss him again. He didn't know that she'd been deliberately avoiding him because of it.

She was finding him easy company. His company wasn't the issue. He wasn't the issue.

She was.

She was still worried she'd give into temptation and kiss him again.

Should she apologise for deliberately staying out of his way this week after revealing so much?

Maybe she should do that right now, she thought. They were alone. There might not be a better time.

She swallowed the red frog, ready to apologise, when two girls burst into the tent supporting a third girl between them.

# CHAPTER FIVE

'OUR FRIEND ISN'T feeling well.'

Molly and Theo hurried over to the girls and ushered them to the back of the marquee. The girl in the middle was unsteady on her feet and Molly doubted she'd be able to stand without the support of her friends. Her eyes were unfocused, her pupils dilated.

'What's her name?' Molly asked.

'Tayla. Tayla Adams.'

'Let's get you up onto the bed,' Molly said as they guided Tayla through the tent to the treatment area at the back. Molly drew the curtain around them to afford some privacy as Theo helped Tayla up onto the examination plinth, physically lifting her when it became apparent that she had neither the coordination nor the comprehension to follow instructions.

'Has she been drinking?' Molly asked. She'd learned over the years never to assume the cause of a patient's symptoms. While she knew it was a fair assumption, there could be other causes, other factors at play.

But Tayla's friends were nodding. 'Vodka shots.'

'How many?'

The two girls looked at each other. 'Maybe ten.'

Molly wasn't certain they were telling the truth. Perhaps they didn't know the answer.

'In how long?'

'Since nine o'clock.'

It was now midnight.

Whatever the number of drinks Tayla had consumed it was obvious she'd drunk more than she could handle. Molly couldn't believe the girl was still standing, let alone conscious.

Molly could see Theo checking Tayla's wrist as she spoke to the friends. She knew he was looking for a medical bracelet or tattoo to indicate an underlying condition. Like her, he wasn't assuming that alcohol alone was responsible for the state Tayla was in. For all they knew she could have diabetes, epilepsy or be on medication that reacted with her alcohol consumption.

'Does Tayla have any allergies or any health problems? Is she diabetic? Epileptic?'

'No.'

'Does she take any prescription medication?'

'No.'

Molly hoped the girls' answers were correct. She looked at their patient, wondering if she should be asking her these questions. But one glance told her that Tayla was not going to be able to help her. Her eyes were glassy. She was conscious, but only just.

'Has she vomited?'

The girls shook their heads. 'She said that her hands and feet were tingling and that she couldn't breathe properly.'

'Has she taken any drugs?'

The girls hesitated. They were looking at each other, avoiding eye contact with Molly.

'It's okay,' Molly told them. 'You need to be honest. We need all the information you can give us in order to help her.'

'She had two caps of MDMA.'

'Temperature forty point two degrees.' Theo had a blood-pressure cuff wrapped around Tayla's arm and was holding a thermometer in her ear. 'Heart rate one hundred and ten.'

Molly knew that ecstasy, the common name for tablets of MDMA, could lead to hyperthermia, especially if Tayla had been dancing, which was highly likely given that most of the festival attendees had been gathered on the beach with the DJ.

'We all had lots of water. Not just the vodka,' the girls added.

Unfortunately that wasn't always the right thing to do. If Tayla's body couldn't process the water it could cause fluid to build up around her brain, which could cause headaches, dizziness, nausea, and even seizures.

'Molly.' Theo's voice held a note of warning. Molly turned around and saw that Tayla's eyes had rolled back in her head. Her mouth was open and Molly could see her tongue had swollen and she was having difficulty breathing.

'Girls, you need to wait outside.' Molly addressed Tayla's friends, who were now crying. She did not have time to deal with them as well. She drew back the curtain and ushered them out, relieved to see that Steph, the volunteer coordinator, was back in the tent. 'Steph, we need an ambulance. Accidental overdose, alcohol and ecstasy. Teenage girl, no significant medical history.'

Steph nodded in reply before Molly retreated back into the cubicle, pulling the curtain closed to block Tayla from her friends' view. She was just in time. Tayla was having a seizure, most likely related to her hyperthermia. There wasn't anything Molly and Theo could do except keep her safe. Theo was on one side of the bed and

Molly quickly stood opposite him, both of them in place to ensure Tayla didn't fall off the bed.

The seizure didn't last long, maybe thirty seconds, but it felt a lot longer. Molly helped Theo to roll Tayla into the recovery position before checking her vital signs again. Her heart rate was still high and her temperature was still elevated. The risk of another seizure was not out of the question.

'Can you grab some wet towels?' Theo asked Molly. He was wedged in behind the treatment plinth and Molly was able to get out more easily. 'We need to try to bring her temperature down.'

'Do you think we should give her a saline drip?' Molly asked when she returned with the damp towels.

Theo shook his head and took a couple of towels from her. Together they draped them over Tayla. 'No. If the seizure was due to cerebral oedema extra fluids could make it worse.' There was no way of knowing whether Tayla's convulsion was related to her temperature or fluid retention around her brain. They were simply making educated guesses and trying to minimise further harm. 'She needs to get to the hospital.'

'I'll check on the ambulance ETA,' Molly said

as they finished laying towels over Tayla. She returned moments later with the paramedics in tow.

Theo did a patient handover as Molly began disconnecting Tayla from the equipment. They reached for the blood-pressure cuff at the same time, Molly's hand coming down a fraction after Theo's, her fingers resting over his. She jerked her hand away but not before she felt the warmth of his skin flow through to her.

Her hand tingled. 'Sorry.'

'Don't be,' Theo replied as he glanced up at her. 'It's fine.' Molly's heart skittered in her chest as her pulse skyrocketed but Theo's eyes told her she had no need to be nervous around him.

She turned away to gather herself together. She was conscious that they weren't alone and disappointed and relieved at the same time. She was a mess of contradictions.

When she wasn't with Theo her resolve was strong. She resolved to be pleasant, friendly but not familiar, but when she was with him, one smile, one accidental touch sent her pulse racing and she forgot that she was going to keep her distance. All she wanted was more of him.

The paramedics had rolled Tayla onto a transfer board as Theo gathered the towels. Together they slid Tayla from the bed to the stretcher and Molly followed the paramedics as they wheeled

Tayla out, giving herself another minute to catch her breath and restore her breathing to its normal pace.

She thought Theo might remain in the treatment area but she was aware that he was behind her. Right behind her. She couldn't see him but she could feel him.

'Is she okay?' Tayla's friends were waiting in the tent and Molly turned her attention to them, letting them distract her, even as she saw Theo move in line with her on the opposite side of the stretcher.

'She should be fine,' Molly told them. 'She's asleep now but she's very lucky to have friends like you.' Molly was talking to the girls but she glanced over at Theo as she spoke. He was watching her with a smile on his face and she knew they were both thinking of the night when he had taken care of her.

Molly smiled back. He had been a good friend to her that night. Something she wasn't sure she deserved. She really did owe him an apology.

'Where are they taking her?' The girls' question brought Molly back to the present.

'To the local hospital. She'll probably need her stomach pumped.'

'Couldn't you give her something to make her vomit?' they asked.

'That's not how we do things now. And Tayla needs to be monitored overnight. She needs to go to hospital. Do you have phone numbers for her parents? They need to be told about what's happened.'

'No.'

'I'll get it sorted,' Steph said as the paramedics opened the rear doors of the ambulance. 'If you girls would like to go to the hospital I'll get one of the Red Frogs to take you,' Steph offered, leaving Molly and Theo free to return to the treatment area.

Molly busied herself tidying up, packing up equipment and throwing away discarded single-use items. The activity meant she could avoid looking at Theo.

'How will Steph find Tayla's parents?' Theo asked.

'The schools all have an emergency contact listed,' she said as she stripped the protective sheet off the treatment plinth. 'Steph can call the number for Tayla's school and they'll get in touch with her parents. It's a bit of a roundabout way to do it but it's better than nothing. Ideally if we had a contact number we could have spoken directly to the parents. Doing it this way means they'll have to call the hospital once they are notified and then chase down the information.'

'We can wait.'

Their shift should have finished an hour ago and Molly was beat. She threw the sheet into the rubbish bin and lifted her gaze to look at Theo. 'It might take them a while to get in contact with Tayla's parents. The hospital will deal with it. I don't know about you but I am exhausted.' She almost said *ready for bed*, but stopped herself at the last minute. She didn't want to complicate things. 'I'm going to head home,' she added right before she collapsed onto the treatment plinth. She lay back and stretched her legs out and let out a big sigh. 'As soon as I can make myself stand up again.'

'Are you hungry? Did you want to grab a cheeseburger from the pub?' he asked.

She shook her head. She was hungry but she didn't feel like negotiating the noise and bustle of the pub. She was exhausted but she knew the adrenalin pumping through her system would keep her awake for hours. Even so, the pub was more than she could handle at the moment. 'I'll make a cup of tea at home. I need peace and quiet. That was a bit hectic.'

Theo held out his hand, offering to help her up. 'Come on, then, I'll walk you to your car.'

She couldn't refuse his hand. That would look odd. She lifted her arm and put her hand in his.

His fingers wrapped around hers. Strong, safe, familiar. He pulled her up as she swung her legs over the side of the bed.

'I didn't drive today,' she said as she stood up, dropping his hand. 'Would you believe I had time to walk?'

Theo smiled and Molly's heart skipped a beat. 'Wonders will never cease.'

'I wish I had driven now,' she admitted. 'I'm not sure I can be bothered walking up the hill.'

'I'll walk home with you, if you like.'

She shook her head. 'You don't need to. I'll be fine.'

'I'm happy to do it. I'd feel better if you let me and, besides, I can pick you up if you collapse with fatigue.' He was still smiling and Molly found she couldn't turn down his offer. She didn't want to. Despite her misgivings, he was easy company, and she was finding she enjoyed spending time with him. She knew it was only her own thoughts that were complicating the situation.

They said goodnight to Steph and left the next shift of volunteers to man the first-aid tent. The beach party was still in full swing and the music followed them up the hill towards Molly's house. She was grateful for the background noise—she was suddenly nervous and the music disguised the lull in conversation, covering their silence.

As they walked further from the centre of town the music and the light faded. Stars shone above them and up ahead the lighthouse stood bright and white and magnificent against the dark sky as it sent its beacon of warning light across the ocean.

'Have you done the lighthouse walk?' Molly asked, desperate to make conversation to fill the emptiness. She felt uncomfortable in the dark and quiet. The silence felt far too intimate. She was afraid she was making herself vulnerable to questions from Theo that she might not want to answer. He seemed to have a knack for getting her to talk about herself and she'd already divulged more to him than she had planned to.

'No, not yet.' Theo's voice was deep, blending into the blackness of the night, and Molly felt it reverberate in her chest.

'You have to make time to do it,' she told him, 'and you should really make sure to get up early to watch the sunrise from there. That's a non-negotiable when you're in Byron. It's a pretty special experience.' The lighthouse building itself was gorgeous but, because the lighthouse stood on the most eastern point of mainland Australia, the view across the Pacific Ocean was amazing.

Theo couldn't leave Byron Bay without making that walk.

'Will you do it with me?'

She'd left herself open to that one. But the idea of watching the sunrise with him appealed to her. It was a magical experience and an iconic Byron Bay activity. She'd just ignore the fact that most people would also consider it a romantic experience. 'Sure,' she replied as they reached her apartment building. 'This is us.'

'Us?'

'Gemma and me,' she said as she entered the code and opened the building's front door. 'I'm going to put the kettle on. Did you want a cup of tea?'

'We won't disturb Gemma?'

Molly shook her head as Theo followed her inside. She headed for the stairs that would take them up to her apartment. 'She's in Brisbane for her grandparents' sixtieth wedding anniversary.'

'That's an impressive achievement.'

'I can't believe people can be happily married for that long,' Molly said as she stepped into her apartment and headed for the kitchen to flick the kettle on.

'You don't think that's normal?'

'Not in my experience.' She'd only seen evidence to the contrary, which was why she was determined not to go down that path. 'Certainly not my parents'. Are yours happily married?'

Theo shrugged. 'Mostly, I think.'

'What's their secret?' she asked as she passed Theo the tea canister, letting him choose his flavour, before filling his mug with boiled water.

'I'd like to say love, but I actually don't know if that's the truth.'

'They don't love each other?'

'I don't know. I've never heard them say they do. I don't remember them telling my sister or me that they loved us either. I guess I've just assumed they do.'

Theo's comments weren't making Molly change her views on marriage. It really didn't have a lot to recommend it, in her opinion.

'So what makes you think they're happy?' she asked.

'They don't seem *unhappy*. They have a lot in common. And common goals. As long as they're achieving those goals, I think they're happy.'

'I think people get comfortable and settle for a situation that perhaps isn't ideal. I know I did,' she admitted. She'd learnt a lot from her relationship with Daniel and she was proud of herself for getting out of it. And she had no intention of putting herself in that position again.

Theo finished his tea and stood up.

'I'm just going to call the hospital and get an update on Tayla,' she said. 'Do you want to wait?'

He nodded but moved from the kitchen and crossed the living room to stand near the front door. Molly wasn't sure if he was giving her space to make the call—he could still hear her talking and she was going to tell him the outcome anyway—or if he was just preparing to leave. She didn't want him to leave. She watched him as she waited for her call to be picked up, afraid to take her eyes off him in case he vanished before she had a chance to say goodnight.

'This is Dr Prescott,' Molly said as her call was answered. 'I sent a patient to the ED via ambulance earlier tonight. I'm just calling for an update. Her name is Tayla Adams.'

Molly had visiting rights at the hospital and she knew the ED staff would be able to tell her the basics of Tayla's condition. That was all she needed to know.

'She's stable,' she told Theo when she finished the call. 'Full of remorse and regret, I suspect, but she's okay.'

'We've all done something we've regretted after a few too many drinks,' Theo replied.

'About that—'

'I'm not talking about you,' Theo said, cutting

Molly off mid-sentence and making her wonder again how he knew what she was thinking.

Molly frowned. 'What did you think I was going to say?'

'You were thinking about the night you kissed me, weren't you?' Molly nodded and Theo continued. 'I was too but I was talking about me. About my regrets.'

'Yours?'

Theo nodded. 'I regret that I walked away. I've always wondered what would have happened if I'd been brave enough to stay.'

'Why didn't you?'

'I expected you to reject me. I didn't believe I deserved you but that didn't stop me wishing and hoping you might see me for who I was. Wishing I'd been braver. Wishing I'd kissed you a second time. I should have had the courage to find out. I was too scared of rejection, of failure, but what was the worst that could have happened? I'd get my heart broken. I was young. It could have been worth it. And I always wish I'd asked you why you kissed me.'

'You want to know why I kissed you?'

He nodded.

'Because you were gorgeous and kind and for the first time I felt like someone was listening to me and that was a powerful thing. Do you remember what you said to me?'

Theo shook his head. 'I wanted to tell you that you had terrible taste in men,' he said, 'but I don't think I did. I didn't think you would listen.'

'I wouldn't have listened,' she admitted with a small smile. 'I *should* have listened but I was determined to make Daniel love me, determined to make him faithful, so I put up with his behaviour and kept going back to him. I saw it as a challenge, something I needed to overcome. I tolerated his behaviour, his treatment of me, instead of walking away because that's what I'd seen my parents doing. Parents can have a lot to answer for. But you're right—you didn't tell me that. Do you remember talking about what we were going to do after graduation?'

'Yes.'

'You were going to work overseas. You told me I should go too. You told me I didn't need to go to work at the hospital in Sydney. I didn't tell you at the time but working overseas sounded exciting. It sounded like an adventure but I knew I wouldn't go. I wasn't brave enough either. I couldn't see myself as separate from Daniel. I made a choice. And then I wondered if you judged me for it. If you found me weak, unambitious, scared, and I was afraid I was all those things.'

'No.' He shook his head. 'I thought you were beautiful and kind and smart and funny and that you deserved so much better than Daniel.'

Molly felt tears well in her eyes as Theo's words washed over her.

'I'm sorry I behaved badly,' she said.

'It's okay. I'm just glad that you finally came to your senses. Even if it did take you a long time,' he said with a smile that took any judgement out of his words.

'I'd invested so much time and effort and energy into the idea of Daniel and me as a couple that it was hard to walk away. And I'm sorry for kissing you. I should have apologised then.' She finally gave the apology that had been haunting her. 'It was a mistake.'

'Was it?'

She shook her head. 'Not the kiss itself. I knew what I was doing. I wanted to kiss you. But it wasn't fair. I was in a relationship and I shouldn't have done it.'

'No. It wasn't fair. But I didn't handle it well,' Theo replied.

They were still standing in her doorway. He was close. If she reached out a hand she could rest it on his chest. It reminded her of this time one week ago. When they'd been standing by her car and she'd resisted the urge to touch him. One part of her knew she'd made the right decision. Another part of her regretted that she'd avoided temptation.

She wanted to touch him.

She wanted to kiss him.

She wanted to ask him to stay.

She wanted a lot of things. None of which she imagined she'd get.

The living room light wasn't on and Theo's dark eyes were hard to read in the dim light. What was he thinking? What did he want? What was he waiting for?

'But we're older and wiser now,' he said. 'And if you wanted to kiss me again it might be different.'

'Really?'

He nodded. Slowly. His gaze was fixed on her face. It was unwavering, steady and calm.

She was a bundle of nerves.

Her head waged a war with her desire. She was taking a break from dating. But she was curious to know what would happen, what a kiss might lead to. And one kiss did not mean they were dating. The chemistry was still there, she didn't think either of them would debate that. There was a spark every time they brushed past one another. With every glance they shared Molly felt as if the rest of the world ceased to exist. Theo could answer questions Molly hadn't even asked. He knew what she was thinking. They had a connection she'd never felt with anyone else.

It was only a kiss.

Her heart was racing. She could feel the blood pounding in her veins, could hear her heart beating.

Was this a bad idea?

She couldn't decide.

Her gaze dropped lower, moving from Theo's eyes to his lips. There was only one way to know for sure.

# CHAPTER SIX

THEO WATCHED MOLLY'S thoughts as they played across her face. He knew the attraction he felt wasn't one-sided. Their connection was real. The chemistry, the buzz he felt when their hands brushed, the buzz he felt when he made her smile, he knew she felt the same.

It had been the same four years ago. They had come together as if they were made for each other. He remembered every detail of that night. He'd tried to forget but seeing her again had brought back every memory—both painful and miraculous.

He'd been foolish to think he could ignore her this time around. The attraction was impossible to ignore.

He had been drawn to Molly from the moment he saw her on their first day at university. He'd waited seven years for her to notice him. Seven years to touch her. Seven years was a long time and the kiss had only made things worse. The kiss they had shared had been amazing but he'd known it wouldn't lead to anything more. And that had been heartbreaking.

Molly and Daniel had had a turbulent relationship but Molly always went back to him and Theo hadn't for one moment thought their one kiss would change anything.

So he'd walked away. Never knowing if things might have turned out differently if he'd stayed, if he'd taken a chance, if he'd kissed her again, if she'd realised that staying with Daniel would be a mistake.

Molly was still looking at him, her lips slightly parted. He could see the tip of her tongue. He watched as she licked her lips, watched as her gaze dropped to his mouth.

He knew she was thinking about kissing him. He just couldn't tell if she would.

He could remember how she had tasted four years ago. She'd tasted of raspberries—sweet, juicy and soft. He wanted to know if she still tasted the same.

He hadn't been brave enough to take a chance four years ago. He needed to be brave now. What was the worst that could happen? She could reject him again, but he'd survived that once before and something was telling him that this time would be different.

He didn't want to wait any longer. It had been four years and six days since he'd last kissed her. That was long enough.

'It's only a kiss,' he said before he dipped his head and claimed her mouth with his.

Molly closed her eyes and parted her lips and a little moan escaped from her throat as she offered herself to him.

Theo accepted her invitation and deepened the kiss, claiming her, exploring. Their first kiss had been tender. Their second was intense. This one was hungry and desperate and demanded a response. She clung to him and he held onto her. He wasn't going to let her go. He lost himself in the warmth of her kiss.

Theo's kiss was commanding, demanding. Gone was the reserved young man. He'd been replaced by a confident man who had seen her desire and could give her what she wanted.

Her heart raced in her chest and she could feel every beat as Theo's lips covered hers. She closed her eyes, succumbing to his touch. She opened her mouth and Theo caressed her tongue. She felt her nipples peak in response as he explored her mouth.

His hands wrapped around her back, the heat of them burning through her T-shirt. She melted against him as her body responded to his touch and a line of fire spread from her stomach to her groin. She deepened the kiss, wanting to lose herself in Theo.

She was aware of nothing else except the sensation of being fully alive. She wanted for nothing except Theo.

His touch was so familiar that it felt like she'd spent a lifetime in his arms. That made no sense but Molly felt as if she belonged there, in his embrace. She felt safe. She felt special. She felt seen.

But the kiss was over way too quickly. Between the hammering of her heart and the heat of Theo's kiss she was completely breathless. She needed to come up for air.

'I should go,' Theo said as they separated.

'You're going to run away again.'

'No. I'm not running. I'm not going anywhere. I'm giving you time to think about what you want. Giving you time to think about whether this is something you want to explore. What happens next is your decision.'

He kissed her again. Lightly this time, the gentlest of touches, so soft she wondered if it was nothing more than her imagination, before he opened the door and said goodnight.

Molly closed the door and leant against it.

Her legs were weak, her knees shaky but her mind was crystal clear, focused, certain. She didn't need time to think. She knew exactly what she wanted. She wanted Theo.

She had wanted the next time to be a mutual decision, consensual. She didn't want to take liberties, didn't want to take advantage, but now she knew Theo wanted it too, wanted her, and she didn't want to give him time to change his mind.

She spun around and flung open the door, desperate to call him back, worried he might have already disappeared.

He was standing right where she'd left him. He hadn't moved.

'You stayed.'

'I stayed.'

'I know what I want,' she told him as she reached out her hand. When he didn't reach for it Molly panicked. Was he going to turn down her offer?

Bu the moment passed and he said, 'You're sure?'

She nodded. She wasn't sure if she would regret her decision but she was prepared to take the chance. At the moment she had two choices—to invite him in or to let him go—and the first option was far more appealing. 'If we find we've made a mistake we can pretend nothing happened,' she said with a smile. 'We know how to do that.'

'We do indeed,' Theo agreed as he took her hand and let her lead him back into her apartment.

Theo pushed the door shut and pulled her to him. He spun her around and she felt the door press against her back. She was grateful for the support as her legs turned to jelly as Theo pressed his lips to the soft spot under her jaw where her pulse throbbed to the beat of her desire.

His lips covered hers as his fingers slid under the fabric of her T-shirt, warm on her skin, setting her on fire. She pulled her shirt over her head, reluctantly breaking the kiss, desperate to feel his skin against hers. She tugged his shirt out of his jeans, pressing her hands into his back.

Theo snapped open the button on her jeans and pushed them to the floor.

'Which one is your room?' he asked.

'Down the hall on the left.'

He picked her up, as though she weighed nothing at all, and Molly wrapped her legs around his waist. She could feel his erection straining against his jeans and she knew he wanted her as urgently as she wanted him.

He kissed her as he carried her to her bedroom and she was astounded that he managed not to crash into any of the walls.

He laid her down on her bed and ran his hand up her thigh. She was wearing only her underwear; he still had far too many clothes on. She reached out to him and slid her hands under his T-shirt, feeling the heat coming off his skin as she dragged his shirt up his back before pulling it over his head.

He bent towards her, kissing the hollow at the base of her neck where her collarbone ended. She tipped her head back and his lips moved down to the swell of her breast. She felt herself arch towards him, silently crying out for his touch. His hand reached behind her and with a flick of his fingers he undid the clasp on her bra and her breasts spilled free. He pushed her back, gently laying her down beneath him before he dipped his head and covered her nipple with his mouth. She closed her eyes as bolts of desire shot from her breasts to her groin. As his tongue caressed her nipple she could feel the moisture gathering between her legs as her body prepared to welcome him.

She heard him snap open the button on his jeans and opened her eyes to watch him divest himself of the rest of his clothing. His erection sprang free as his clothes hit the floor. He knelt between her legs and she slid her hands behind his back and ran them down over his buttocks. They were round and hard under her palms.

Theo moved his attention to her other breast as she moved one hand between his legs, cupping his testicles before running her hand along the length of his shaft. She heard him moan as her fingers rolled across the tip, using the moisture she found there to decrease the friction and smooth her movements.

She arched her hips towards him and he responded, removing her knickers and sliding his fingers inside her. She gasped as he circled her most sensitive spot with his thumb. He was hard and hot under her palm; she was warm and wet to his touch.

She was ready now. She didn't want to wait. She couldn't wait.

She opened her legs and guided him into her, welcoming the full length of him.

He pushed against her and she lifted her hips to meet his thrust. They moved together, matching their rhythms as if they'd been doing this for ever. She had her hands at his hips, controlling the pace, gradually increasing the momentum. Theo's breaths were short and Molly didn't think she was breathing at all. All her energy was focused on making love to him. There was no room in her head for anything other than the sensation of his skin against hers, his skin inside hers.

Theo gathered her hands and held them above her head, stretching her out and exposing her breasts, and he bent his head to her nipple again as he continued his thrusts. She wrapped her legs around him, binding them together. The energy they created pierced through her, flowing from his mouth, through her breast and into her groin where it gathered in a peak of pleasure building with intensity until she thought she would explode.

'Now, Theo, do it now,' she begged.

His pace increased a fraction more and as she felt him start to shudder, she released her hold as well. Their timing was exquisite, controlled by the energy that flowed between them, and they cried out in unison, climaxing simultaneously.

Their bodies had been made for each other and their coupling had been everything Molly had expected and more. They had been unified by their lovemaking and it was an experience Molly would treasure for ever.

Molly had fallen asleep with Theo curled against her and she woke up in the same position. Theo's hand cupped her bare breast. His breath was warm on her shoulder. He was breathing deeply, still asleep, but Molly needed to use the bathroom. She lifted his hand from her breast and slid out of bed, moving slowly, trying not to wake him.

She went to the bathroom and then looked for her phone. She checked the time even though there was nothing she needed to do today. It had been late when they'd fallen asleep and it was late now, almost eleven in the morning. She plugged her phone in to charge in the kitchen—it had spent the night on the lounge room floor in the pocket of her jeans and was almost out of power—and flicked the kettle on before going back to the bedroom.

Theo was awake and Molly was suddenly overcome with a bout of nerves. What if he had regrets about last night?

He greeted her with a wide smile and she relaxed. 'Good morning,' she said.

'It's a very good morning,' Theo agreed as he reached for her and pulled her back into bed.

He ran his fingers up her thigh, cupping the curve of her bottom. Molly closed her eyes and arched her hips, pushing herself closer to him. He bent his head and kissed her. She opened her mouth, joining them together. Theo ran his hand over her hip and up across her stomach, his fingers grazing her breasts. He watched as her nipple peaked under his touch and she moaned softly and reached for him, but he wasn't done yet.

He flicked his tongue over one breast, sucking it into his mouth. He supported himself on one elbow while he used his other hand in tandem with his mouth, teasing her nipples until both were taut with desire. He slid his knee between her thighs, parting them as he straddled her. His right hand stayed cupped over her left breast as he moved his mouth lower to kiss her stomach.

He took his hand from her breast and ran it up the smooth skin of the inside of her thigh. She moaned and thrust her hips towards him as her knees dropped further apart.

'Patience, Molly. Relax and enjoy,' he said, and his voice was muffled against the soft skin of her hip bone.

Theo put his head between her thighs. He put his hands under her bottom and lifted her to his mouth, supporting her there as his tongue darted inside her. She knew she was slick and wet, and she moaned as he explored her inner sanctum with his tongue. She thrust her hips towards him again, urging him deeper.

He slid his fingers inside her as he sucked at

her swollen sex. His fingers worked in tandem with his tongue, making her pant, making her beg for more.

'Theo, please. I want you inside me.'

But Theo wasn't ready to stop. Not yet. He had waited years for this. He wanted to taste her, to feel her orgasm. He knew she was close to climaxing and he wanted to bring her to orgasm like this. He knew this was a skill he possessed.

He ignored her request as he continued to work his magic with his tongue, licking and sucking the swollen bud of her desire. He continued until Molly had forgotten her request, until she had forgotten everything except her own satisfaction.

'Yes, yes… Oh, Theo, don't stop.'

He had no intention of stopping.

He heard her sharp little intake of breath and then she began to shudder.

'Yes. Oh, Theo.'

She buried her fingers in his hair and clamped her thighs around his shoulders as she came, shuddering and gasping before she collapsed, relaxed and spent.

'God, you're good at that,' she said, and he could hear the smile and contentment in her voice.

'Thank you.' He lay alongside her, his hand resting on her stomach as she cuddled into him.

He felt her hand on the shaft of his penis. 'Now it's your turn,' she said as she slid her hand up and down. 'And I want to feel you inside me. Please?'

'Seeing as you asked so nicely,' he replied as he gave himself up to Molly's rhythm.

She cupped his testes with one hand as the other encircled his shaft. Theo could feel it pulsing with a life of its own as Molly ran her hand up its length. She rolled her fingers over the end and coaxed the moisture from his body. Theo gasped and his body trembled.

She sat up and straddled his hips.

'Give me a second,' he said. He rolled onto his side, careful not to dislodge Molly, and found his jeans lying on the floor by the bed. He pulled his wallet from the pocket and retrieved a condom. He opened the packet and rolled it on in one smooth, fast movement.

Molly sat above him, naked and glorious, and Theo felt another rush of blood to his groin as she brought herself forward and raised herself up onto her knees before lowering herself onto him. Theo closed his eyes and sighed as she took his length inside her.

She lifted herself up again, and down, as Theo

held onto her hips and started to time her thrusts, matching their rhythms together. Slow at first and then gradually faster. And faster.

'Yes. Yes.'

'Harder.'

'Oh, God, yes, that's it.'

He had no idea who was saying what, all he knew was he didn't want it to stop.

'Now. Yes. Keep going. Don't stop.'

Just when he thought he couldn't stand it any longer he felt Molly start to quiver and he let himself go too, breathing out as his orgasm joined hers in perfect harmony. She was insatiable but their timing couldn't have been better.

They lay together looking up at the ceiling, breathing heavily as they recovered before Molly sat up suddenly, the sheet falling to her waist as she turned to look at Theo, a horrified expression on her face. 'We didn't use any protection last night!'

It had been the last thing on his mind. And obviously on hers too. They'd been too focused on their needs and desires, ignoring all practicalities.

Theo could feel the colour drain from his face. He sat up. 'You're not on any contraception?' he asked. 'Not that I'm saying it's your responsibility.'

Molly shook her head. 'I stopped taking the pill when I moved here.'

Damn. He'd been so caught up in the moment last night that he hadn't even made assumptions about contraception. He hadn't even stopped to think. 'I'm sorry. We should have had that conversation. I've let you down.'

'We're both to blame,' Molly replied, sharing the responsibility. 'I certainly didn't stop to think.'

'What would you like to do?' he asked. 'Do you want to take a morning-after pill?'

That was their best option. It wasn't perfect by any means, but it was their only choice.

Molly nodded.

'I'll go and get one,' he offered. 'And I should get more condoms too if we're going to keep doing this.'

'Are we going to keep doing this?' she asked.

'Why wouldn't we? I enjoyed it. And I hope you did too. There's no reason that I can think of to stop.' He picked up her hand and kissed her fingers, one by one.

'I'm supposed to be finding myself,' she said, 'not getting into another relationship.'

'I'm only here for four more weeks. I don't think a few weeks would qualify as a relationship.'

'Plenty of people have relationships that last less than that.'

'Well then, maybe it just depends on what we want to call it? What about hot, steamy, no-strings, no-commitment sex? Is that off limits too?'

Theo was smiling and despite the situation Molly found him impossible to resist. 'I hadn't thought about it, but you've made me realise that I miss sex.'

'I don't think you should deprive yourself, then. If it will help you sleep better at night, why don't we call it a holiday romance?'

'Neither of us are on holiday though,' she argued with a smile.

'Friends with benefits? A summer fling?' he proposed.

Molly shook her head. 'I can't think while I'm naked.'

'All right, then, you can get back to me on that. I'll go to the pharmacy now and when I come back I'll take you out for lunch.'

'You don't need to go to the pharmacy. Go to the clinic. There'll be morning-after pills in the dispensary cabinet. Do you have a key for that?'

'Yes. Do I need to sign it out?'

Molly shook her head. 'No. And there will be condoms in the nurses' room, just in case we get carried away again. They give them out at the safe sex talks they run.'

A wide grin lit up Theo's face. 'Maybe we should sign up for those.'

He kissed her before he got out of bed, affording Molly a very nice view of his bare backside as he retrieved his clothes. 'I'll go to the clinic, duck home for a shower and come back for you.'

Molly stretched her arms and legs out and felt several muscles complain. Despite her regular swims and her walks up to the lighthouse there were some muscles that obviously hadn't had a thorough workout for a while. Her sheets smelt of sex and she probably did too. But she didn't mind—the sex had been amazing and she was glad she'd given in to the temptation. It had been worth breaking her temporary vow of celibacy.

Theo had been worth it.

She finished stretching and, with a smile on her face, headed for the shower. But her smile faded as she remembered their lack of contraception. The morning-after pill worked by delaying ovulation by several days but her menstrual cycle was irregular and she had no idea where she was at. She crossed her fingers and hoped everything would be okay. Not every instance of unprotected sex resulted in a pregnancy, she reminded herself. It would be fine.

# CHAPTER SEVEN

THEO STRETCHED HIS legs under the table and managed, with some difficulty, to keep a wide smile off his face. He felt good, last night and this morning with Molly had been spectacular, and he felt as if he'd won the lottery. He'd suspected he and Molly had a chemistry that was off the charts, not that he had much to compare it to, his relationship history being limited to one semi-serious one and a few short-lived, casual romances. He prided himself on being a considerate lover and knew how to please women, but he preferred it when there wasn't too much expected of him from an emotional viewpoint. He wasn't sure if he possessed those skills. That was a work in progress.

But Molly made him want to try. He imagined she would be worth it.

But he was only in Byron Bay for four more weeks. What could he achieve in that time? When he had returned from the clinic earlier this morning Molly had agreed to a summer romance, but Theo suspected that wouldn't be enough for him. Not after last night.

He breathed deeply, inhaling the orange fragrance of Molly's shampoo. He was relaxed, he wasn't thinking about work, his mind was still and quiet, which was a rarity for him. Molly's presence today was calming on his mind if not on his libido.

He wanted to celebrate but Molly didn't seem to share quite the same level of enthusiasm. He was enjoying his lunch but Molly's lack of appetite suggested she had something on her mind. The table next to them at the little café in Brunswick Heads was occupied by a family with two small children and her gaze kept flitting towards the slightly frazzled mother and the toddler in a high chair.

'Is everything okay?' he asked.

'God, I hope so,' Molly replied as her gaze flicked, yet again, to the table beside them before she turned back to face Theo, concern in her blue-grey eyes. 'I really don't want kids.'

That was a segue he hadn't expected and her comment surprised him. She sounded so adamant. 'Not at all?' he asked.

'I don't think so. Certainly not right now.'

'You and Daniel didn't talk about it?' He

wasn't sure if it was wise to bring Daniel's name into the conversation, but Molly had dated him for years and Theo was curious to know how serious they had really been.

Molly shook her head. 'Never.'

Theo looked across to the family at the adjacent table. The toddler smiled in his direction and Theo smiled back and then pulled a funny face.

Molly watched him. 'Do you want kids?'

He nodded. None of his past relationships had ever progressed to the point where he could see a future, where he could imagine starting a family, but that hadn't meant he didn't want one. He was hopeful that, one day, he'd fall in love, get married and have children. In his heart, he believed he could love and be loved and he wanted, one day, to have a family of his own.

'Why?' she asked, and he tried to ignore the slightly incredulous tone in her question.

'I want to be able to love someone unconditionally.' In his mind that was a partner and children. It was a dream he'd had but never voiced. Until now. 'I think having kids could be tremendously fulfilling and rewarding if you have them for the right reasons.'

'I'm not so sure,' Molly disagreed. 'The way I see it, mothers in particular have to sacrifice their freedom and independence to raise a family and I'm only just getting mine back. I lost sight of my independence when I was with Daniel and I have no intention of giving it up again any time soon.'

Molly was rubbing the palm of her hand with her opposite thumb in a nervous gesture. Her frown was creased, her worry obvious.

'Well, if it makes you feel any better, the chances of getting pregnant from one episode of unprotected sex are slim, and even slimmer considering you've taken the morning-after pill,' Theo said, knowing what was on her mind and trying to calm her fears. He kept his voice low, conscious of the family at the next table, and tried to pretend that her thoughts didn't bother him.

She was being honest, and he had to acknowledge and appreciate that, but her opinion surprised him and raised the first question mark in his mind. He'd pictured himself with a wife and kids one day. He didn't have a specific timeframe; he knew that was a luxury of being a male. But it was something he wanted in his future, and hearing Molly's thoughts made him wonder if perhaps they weren't as compatible as he'd like to believe.

He reminded himself they had agreed only

to a summer romance. Their compatibility past Christmas was irrelevant.

But, after last night, he wondered how hard it was going to be to say goodbye and relegate her to his past. Again.

Molly had chosen to take Theo to Brunswick Heads, fifteen minutes north of Byron Bay, for lunch. She told him it was to avoid the Schoolies Festival but, in the back of her mind, she thought it was a sensible choice. Going out in Byron, they were bound to run into someone she knew and she wasn't ready to explain why they were having lunch together.

The café she'd chosen was one of her favourites but being seated next to a young family had freaked her out a little, making her head ache with thoughts of 'what if?'. A post-lunch walk along the beach, hand in hand with Theo, the sound of the waves crashing on the sand and the feeling of the salt spray and sun on her face, had gradually calmed her mind until she felt confident that all would be well, and by the time they headed back to Byron she was feeling less panicked and more like her normal self.

She pointed out landmarks to Theo as she drove them back to town, slowing down as she approached an intersection on a narrow road as another car was headed towards them from the opposite direction. As she eased off the accelerator there was a flash of movement, a flash of red, to her right.

All of a sudden the flash of red became a person on an e-scooter. Molly saw him look to his left before careening straight onto the road. Straight into the path of the other car that was approaching from his right. The car had no time to swerve and only barely enough time to slam on its brakes. But even that wasn't enough to enable the driver to avoid the impact.

Molly hit the brakes instinctively and watched in horror as the scooter rider bounced off the other car's bonnet and was flung into the air before crashing onto the road in front of Molly's now stationary car. Thank God she'd stopped—if she hadn't she would have run straight over him.

Molly and Theo sprang from the car and rushed to the rider's side.

A second rider, a female, dropped her scooter on the footpath and ran into the middle of the road, screaming.

The driver of the car that had hit him raced over. 'Is he all right? He came from nowhere. I didn't have time to stop.'

'I know,' Molly said. The driver was obviously in shock and understandably concerned. 'We saw the whole thing. He looked the wrong way. He didn't see you.'

The rider's eyes were open, his expression suggested he was wondering what had happened, but at least he was conscious and breathing. He'd been wearing a helmet and that was still fastened under his chin. He was lucky. Most scooter riders Molly saw didn't bother with a helmet, even though the law required them to wear one. It might have just saved this man's life.

'Don't move,' Theo said as it looked as if the man might attempt to get up. 'We're doctors, let us check you over first.'

The man, who was of Asian appearance, frowned as he looked at Theo, but didn't reply. Did he have a concussion or did he not understand the question? Molly wondered.

He looked at the young girl who was squatting beside him and spoke to her in a foreign language that sounded to Molly like Mandarin.

To her surprise, Theo replied.

She'd had no idea he spoke a second language. It just reminded her of how little she knew about him.

She sat by as a spectator as Theo, the rider and the young woman had a conversation. The man was gesturing to his right arm and shoulder.

Theo was speaking now, his words accompanied by hand gestures. He opened and closed his fist before bending and straightening his elbow. The injured man copied Theo's movements, somewhat hesitantly, but he was able to complete the two actions.

Next, Theo demonstrated lifting his arm away from his body but the young man shook his head. He said a few words but Molly couldn't tell if he was refusing or unable to perform that movement.

He pointed to the tip of his shoulder where the collarbone and shoulder blade met.

'What's he saying?' Molly asked.

'It hurts to move his shoulder.'

Theo spoke to the young man again but without any accompanying actions. The man nodded and Theo ran his hands gently over the man's clavicle and shoulder blade.

Molly watched. Theo's hands were gentle, his fingers long and slender. Just a few hours ago those same hands had been tangled in her hair, cupping her breasts, between her legs, bringing her to orgasm. She closed her eyes. What was the expression? Still waters run deep. She'd always thought of Theo as being reserved but she'd definitely seen a different side to him last night and this morning. He was passionate, considerate and was it any wonder she'd found herself agreeing to a summer fling? She wasn't about to deny herself a few weeks of pleasure.

Theo spoke and then translated for Molly. 'I think he's fractured his clavicle. Can you call for an ambulance? And then we need to get him off the road.'

Molly's phone was in her car. She went to fetch it, moving her car to the side of the road in the process, while Theo helped the man, whose name was Leung, to his feet. Theo brought him over to Molly's car and let him sit in it to wait for the ambulance.

Molly dialled 000, gave their location, and explained there had been a car versus e-scooter accident.

'They're sending an ambulance and a police car,' she said as she hung up. The police would breath-test the driver of the car involved as well as Leung. Molly suspected Theo would need to explain that process too. Theo was still talking to Leung but Molly could recognise only a few words—'Byron Bay', mostly.

Theo gave a patient handover when the paramedics arrived and Molly got more information then.

'We have a twenty-four-year-old male who was riding an e-scooter when he collided with a car. He has injured his right shoulder, suspected fractured clavicle.'

The paramedics asked a question, which Theo relayed to Leung and then repeated the answer, in English, to the paramedics. 'Yes, he has travel insurance.'

Another question. Another translation. Another response, 'No allergies.'

'Will there be a translator at the hospital?' Theo asked as the paramedics prepared to put Leung onto a stretcher.

'If there's not then the hospital use a dial-in translator over the phone,' the paramedics explained.

The police arrived and Theo gave them a description of the events before they breath-tested the involved parties. The crisis over and their patient strapped securely to the stretcher, Theo and Molly were finally free to head off.

'I could use a beer,' Theo said. 'Shall we go to my place? It's only around the corner.'

They got back in her car and Molly followed his directions, driving through town and onto Childe Street where Theo's accommodation was one of a dozen or so houses. It was single storey, tucked in among the sand dunes. Theo led Molly past three bedrooms and a bathroom, a simple layout with pale wooden floors and white walls, but Molly's jaw dropped as she stepped from the passage into an open-plan kitchen living space. The back wall of the house was glass and over the top of a low hedge of native plants Molly could see the ocean. The water looked to be mere steps from the back door. Theo unlocked the large glass door and slid it back, connecting the house to a deck that led straight onto the sand. Molly could see a narrow path stretching between the salt bush giving direct access to Belongil Beach.

She was drawn to the deck and stood taking in the view. It was the same ocean that she could see from her house, but standing here it felt as if the sea were close enough to touch, as if she could reach out a hand and dip it in the water from the comfort of the house. It would be incredible to live somewhere like this. It felt a million miles away from the busyness of Main Beach.

'This is amazing. I had no idea these houses were here,' she said as Theo reappeared holding two beers he'd fetched from the fridge. He passed one to her and she took it and sat on the end of a sun lounger, facing the ocean.

'It's pretty incredible,' he said. 'I've come to love this spot in the past few weeks. Nothing beats sitting on the deck with a beer at the end of the day, watching the waves roll in. Well, almost nothing,' he added with a grin and Molly knew instinctively that he was referring to last night.

Theo took a seat behind her, straddling the sun lounger, and Molly leant on him, resting her back against his chest. 'How on earth did you find this place?'

Theo wrapped his arms around her and Molly relaxed into his embrace. 'A friend of my sister's owns it. She's overseas. She doesn't rent it out but she lets friends and family use it. I think she was pleased to have someone in it during the Schoolies Festival.'

She closed her eyes and listened to the waves breaking on the shore. She could hear the sea from her house if the windows were open, but here it sounded as if the water were lapping at her feet. The real world receded into the distance as she lost herself in the sounds of the sea, the tang of the salt air, the warmth of the sun on her face and the touch of Theo's hands on her skin.

Molly caught the yeasty smell of Theo's beer as he sipped his drink. She'd forgotten all about hers.

'I had no idea you spoke a second language,' Molly said. 'That you are fluent in Mandarin.'

'You know I'm mixed race, right?'

'Of course.'

'My dad is Australian; my mum is Taiwanese. She moved to Australia from Taiwan to finish her schooling, met my dad at university when they were both studying medicine and they married. I grew up speaking English and Mandarin. Mum's parents moved here when my sister and I were little to look after us, basically, while Mum and Dad worked. We grew up speaking Mandarin with them.'

'You said both your parents are doctors.'

'Dad is a plastic surgeon and Mum is a GP. Lian Chin.'

Molly frowned. 'Lian Chin. That's the same name as the doctor who owns Pacific Coast Clinics.' She sat up and spun around to face Theo.

Theo nodded. 'That's my mum.'

'You're the boss's son? Why didn't you say anything?'

'Why does it matter? It's not relevant. Is it?'

Molly hesitated. It felt very relevant. It felt as if he was hiding something. Why wouldn't he have told people? Told her? That was the real question. She frowned. 'Why didn't you tell me?'

'I just did.'

'I meant, why didn't you tell me earlier?'

'I don't want people to think I got where I am because I'm related to the boss.'

‘Can you honestly tell me that’s not why you’re here?’

‘The staff in Sydney were asked if anyone wanted to cover here for Tom’s leave. Being so close to Christmas, no one did. I am here because no one else put their hand up so, as the boss’s son, I had to fill the gap. But I didn’t want to be judged by my name or by my relationship to Lian. My surname is officially Chin Williams but, because it isn’t hyphenated, I usually just go by Williams. It was a habit I developed in high school, a strategy to help me fit in, to seem less Asian.’

Molly sensed there was more to this situation than Theo was telling her, but she let him continue rather than pushing for him to disclose more.

‘All my life I’ve been judged on my achievements,’ Theo continued. ‘My results at school and university. My contribution. I’ve been expected to excel and been criticised if I fall short. I’ve never been praised for the person I am, only for what I’ve done. I don’t want to be seen as the boss’s son. I want people to see me. Theo. Can you understand that?’

Molly was nodding her head. ‘I can. I wanted my father to see me and so I created a personality for myself—a persona—to try to make me stand out from the crowd. It became a protective mechanism. I became the person I wanted people to see. Now I'm just trying to be me. The best me I can be. So, yes, I know what it's like to feel invisible, to be judged or misjudged.'

Theo's phone buzzed with a text message.

'It's from Matt,' he said as he read it. 'Inviting me for a barbecue dinner tonight.' He sounded surprised.

'That's nice,' Molly said. It was, but she wasn't sure how she felt about it.

'You don't sound convinced. What's the catch?'

It was one thing agreeing to have a summer romance or to being friends with benefits, it was another thing spending time together in public. Did she want everyone to know what they were doing?

She knew she didn't. Just as she believed Theo's business was his, hers was hers. 'There's no catch,' she said. 'Matt and Levi host a regular Sunday night barbecue. Gemma and I usually go.'

'Are you going tonight?'

She nodded.

'Shall we go together?'

Theo didn't seem to have the same concerns as her. He seemed quite comfortable with the fact that they were sleeping together but that didn't make them a couple. They'd agreed to being friends with benefits. Did that mean that everyone else had to know what they were doing or could they keep it between themselves? How did she want to play this relationship in public? Because, no matter what they called it, and even if it was only going to be short-lived, it was a relationship of sorts. She had never had a one-night stand and anything more than that had to have some level of connection, didn't it?

What had she agreed to exactly?

'I need to go home and change. Can I meet you there?' she stalled to avoid answering his question directly. 'Their place is halfway between here and home.' She wanted to keep their dalliance between them. She didn't want to share it, she didn't want to talk about it, she didn't want to discuss it and she didn't want to hear everyone's opinions on the subject. She didn't want the others to know.

Theo nodded. He either didn't notice her hesitation or he chose to ignore it.

The night had started off well. Theo had noted that Molly had avoided arriving with him but that hadn't bothered him. This 'thing' between them was new and they hadn't discussed what, if anything, they were going to tell people. But when everyone was discussing their weekends and Molly completely wiped him from her recount, with the exception of their shift at the Schoolies Festival, he couldn't help but feel slighted. He didn't expect her to share every intimate detail with her friends, but did it matter if they knew Molly and he had gone out for lunch? Why was she pretending the day hadn't happened? Was he not good enough for her? Was he something, someone, she wanted to keep secret?

And could he be upset with her if she *was* keeping secrets?

He was keeping secrets too. He couldn't in complete honesty say that his presence in Byron Bay had nothing to do with being a Chin Williams. His mother had requested he go to Byron Bay on her behalf. He'd told a half-truth. He certainly hadn't told Molly the whole story.

He took his guitar out onto the deck when he got home and wasn't surprised to hear that the first few chords he played had a melancholy note.

Would he ever be good enough?

Would he ever be good enough for Molly?

The sad notes kept coming, his fingers seeming to find them of their own accord.

Was he prepared to be a closely guarded secret?

Was Molly worth the angst?

He was only in Byron for another month. Should he walk away now? Save himself from inevitable heartbreak?

No. He'd walked away before and regretted it, he thought as the chords he played became stronger, more determined. Failure no longer had the same hold over him. He was willing to take a chance. Molly was worth a shot. He was still fascinated by her, intrigued by her, attracted to her, and he wouldn't walk away again.

'Theo?' The intercom on his clinic phone buzzed and he heard Paula's voice. 'Do you have time to see a walk-in patient? I have an eighteen-year-old male here who's complaining of abdominal pain.'

'Sure. I'll come and get him.' Theo was pleased to fill up his diary. Too much time on his hands meant too much time to sit and think about Molly. He was still trying to figure out what had been going through her mind last night, and getting nowhere, so more work was a welcome distraction. He didn't even mind that this was exactly the sort of patient who should be presenting to the hospital ED or even the Schoolies Festival first-aid tent which was open for its last day rather than the medical clinic. As long as he was prepared to pay for a consult.

That thought reminded him again of Molly—their first shared patient, Warwick with the cardiac arrest. He hadn't been charged for his consult, but Theo needed to remember that not everything was about money. He'd become a doctor because he wanted to help people. He had worked overseas after finishing uni, in Third World countries—he definitely wasn't about the money—but he knew his mother wouldn't be happy about giving their expertise away for free. Not if patients could afford to pay for their services.

'Will?' He called for his patient.

A teenage boy stood up slowly from a chair in the corner of the waiting room, slightly unsteady on his feet. He had his right arm held across his stomach and as he stood he reached out with his left hand to stabilise himself on the wall.

'Are you okay?' Theo asked, even though it was obvious the answer was no.

'Just a bit dizzy.'

He was tall and lanky, his face pale. He was flanked by a couple of friends, one of whom put an arm around his waist and lent him support. Theo looked at the group. 'You're here for the Schoolies Festival?' They looked about the right age and all looked a little worse for wear, as if they'd had a late night and hadn't had enough coffee or fried food yet to cure their hangovers.

Will looked worse than the rest. Unable to stand up straight, his face pale and drawn, he was obviously in pain. It looked as if he was suffering from more than a simple hangover.

Theo let Will's mates help him into the examination room but ushered them out once Will was lying on the treatment bed. He seemed coherent and was able to understand Theo's conversation. He'd call the other boys back if he needed them.

'What seems to be the trouble, Will?' he asked after introducing himself.

'I've got some discomfort in my stomach, just here.' He was holding his hand over the left side of his abdomen, just below his ribs.

'Sharp or stabbing pain like a knife or tenderness like a bruise?' Theo asked.

'Like a bruise. But there's no bruise I can see.'

'You're dizzy as well?' Theo checked, recalling his comment from the waiting room.

Will nodded and then closed his eyes, the movement of his head obviously unsettling him. 'That could have something to do with my hangover.'

'When did you last have an alcoholic drink?'

'Last night probably about ten o'clock.' That

was twelve hours ago. 'I wasn't feeling too good then. We'd been drinking since lunch and I started feeling a bit off.'

Theo wasn't surprised. But he needed a better explanation as to Will's symptoms. 'Off?'

'Dizzy. I thought I'd had too much to drink.'

'And when did you first notice the tenderness?'

'This morning.'

Theo clipped an oximeter to Will's finger and then took his blood pressure.

'I was wondering if I could have alcohol poisoning?' Will asked. 'Would that give me stomach pain?'

Theo assumed Will had consulted Dr Google and wondered if he should advise him against it. 'That would be likely to make you nauseous but unlikely to present as tenderness in a specific area unless you'd strained a stomach muscle through vomiting. Have you vomited? Had any difficulty breathing? Lost consciousness in the past twelve hours?'

'No.' Will shook his head.

His blood pressure was lower than normal and his heart rate was rapid.

'I need to have a look at your skin. Can you lift your T-shirt up for me?'

Will pulled his T-shirt up, exposing his abdomen. His skin was unblemished. It was lightly tanned but not enough to camouflage any bruising.

'I'm just going to feel your abdominal organs.'

Theo started on the right, gently palpating Will's liver before moving across to the left side. His appendix didn't appear to be giving him any discomfort and Theo reached across Will and lifted the left ribcage slightly with his left hand before pressing his right hand in and up under the ribs. 'Can you breathe in for me?'

The spleen moved down, allowing him to feel the inferior margin. That was a little concerning. The spleen wasn't normally palpable except in very thin adults. If they breathed in the spleen could pop out from under the ribcage.

There were a few red flags, the elevated heart rate, low blood pressure and abdominal tenderness, but they could just as easily indicate side effects of a few days of hard partying as Will celebrated the end of his schooldays.

'Have you had a knock or blow to your stomach in the past couple of days?'

'We were playing beer-can jousting yesterday and we got knocked over and one of the girls fell and landed on me. Her knee went into my stomach. I didn't think anything of it until this morning. I looked for a bruise but I couldn't see anything.'

Theo had a sense that something else was at play.

'I'm just going to lie the bed flat,' he said as he stepped on the control pad to lower the back of the bed and prepared to do an additional test. 'I want you to lift both your legs into the air and tell me if you feel any discomfort with that movement.'

Will did as he was instructed and Theo saw him wince as he lifted his legs. Will grabbed at his left shoulder, reinforcing Theo's interim diagnosis.

'I think you might have damaged your spleen,' he told him. While Will's symptoms matched any number of things, that last test was quite specific and, combined with the other results, Theo was fairly certain he was looking at signs of a damaged spleen.

'I'd like to send you to the hospital for some tests.'

'What sort of tests?'

'A CT scan to check for damage to your spleen caused by blunt force trauma, for example, someone landing forcefully with their knee on your spleen, and an ultrasound to check for blood in the abdominal cavity. I just need to get an assessment organised.'

Theo wanted to send Will for a specialist opinion, but he had no idea whether it was something that the hospital could provide or if he needed to send his patient to a larger town with better access to specialist clinics. Gemma wasn't at work yet. He would need to ask Molly for advice.

'I have a teenage boy, a Schoolies participant, who has presented with abdominal tenderness and dizziness,' he told her when he found her in the staffroom. 'I'm concerned that he's damaged his spleen.'

'Are you sure? There are several things that present with similar symptoms.'

'I know, but there's one fairly specific test, which was positive,' he said before explaining the test.

Molly frowned. 'I've never heard of that test. How did you know about it?'

'When I was working in Cambodia and Indonesia there were lots of scooter accidents. It was fairly common to patients presenting with abdominal pain after getting handlebars in the abdomen. I was shown that test over there. We probably saw more than the average number of damaged spleens over there, caused by the blunt trauma of a handlebar into the spleen, and that test was pretty reliable. Unfortunately, there wasn't the same access we have here to scans, diagnostic tests or even blood tests. If we suspected spleen damage it was a case of monitoring and hoping that it was minor enough that it would resolve. Non-surgical intervention was our usual treatment option. Often our only treatment option. But what I wanted to know was whether I can send Will to hospital here for further tests. Can we make that referral?'

Molly nodded. 'There are general surgeons at the hospital. Make a phone call and advise that you're sending a patient for scans and review. Is he here with friends?'

'Yes.'

'If he's not critical then he can call an Uber and go with friends.'

'Okay. Thank you. Have you got another minute?' he asked, waylaying her as she was about to leave.

She waited.

'Is everything okay between us?'

'What do you mean?'

'Last night. I thought we'd have a good time together. I thought we'd agreed to a summer fling but then you brushed me off and brushed over our weekend. As if you were embarrassed.

If you're having second thoughts, please just tell me. I'd rather you were honest with me.'

Molly shook her head. 'I'm not having second thoughts, I did have a good time, but the whole thing was a bit unexpected. I didn't know how to behave and it made me self-conscious. I didn't say anything because I didn't want people to think we were in a relationship. I don't want to be in a relationship.'

'We agreed to keep it casual,' Theo said. 'Don't worry about what other people think. All that matters is how we feel. If you're not having a good time, we call it quits, okay?'

Molly nodded.

'And don't feel you have to include me in everything you do,' he continued. 'We're not dating, we're just having fun. Let's just relax and enjoy the next few weeks and make some memories. If you need space, just tell me. Promise you will talk to me, that you'll tell me if there's a problem.'

'Okay.'

# CHAPTER EIGHT

MOLLY'S ALARM BUZZED, rousing her from her sleep. She reached for her phone to hit snooze, disturbing Theo in the process.

He rolled over and pulled her into him, holding her close.

He kissed her shoulder. His lips were warm and soft. He trailed his hand from her hip down her thigh and up again, sliding his hand between her legs. Molly shifted her weight and opened her legs. She seemed to be constantly aroused when she was with Theo. A glance, a smile and especially a touch of his hand, even the lightest of touches, all had the power to trigger her libido. And there was no denying how compatible they were in bed. But outside the bedroom they had been getting on just as well. Molly enjoyed Theo's company. She used to feel he was judging the old Molly—although it turned out she was her harshest critic—but she got no sense of judgement any more. He was happy in her company, as she was in his.

And she had decided that there was no point pretending otherwise. They were seeing each other casually and she'd admitted as much to her friends. She and Theo had no expectations of each other of anything bigger, anything permanent, so there really was no need to hide their summer romance from anyone. She'd been slightly surprised to find her friends were all unanimously positive in their support of the romance, but Molly had stressed that it wasn't going to be anything serious—their affair would be over almost before it began. A line would be drawn through it when Theo returned to Sydney.

She wasn't thinking about how she would feel then—she still didn't like to examine her feelings too closely. She was still telling herself it was a summer fling, although she was worried she was in deeper than she'd planned to be.

Theo's fingers were working their magic and Molly forgot about the alarm she'd set until the snooze button went off. Reluctantly she covered Theo's hand with hers and stilled his movements.

'What's the matter?' he asked.

She rolled over and apologised with a kiss.

'Nothing. But if we want to see the sunrise we need to get up.'

'It's still dark,' Theo complained. 'I'd rather stay in bed with you. There will be another sunrise tomorrow.'

'It's forecast to rain tomorrow,' Molly said. 'You can't come to Byron and not see the sunrise from the lighthouse at least once. We can come back to bed after our walk.'

'Is that a promise?'

She nodded and kissed him again before throwing off the covers and pulling him out of bed. They did need to get going if they were going to make it up the track before sunrise.

Molly and Theo leant on the white wooden fence at the top of the hill. The lookout was almost deserted save for a couple of other early risers. The lighthouse stood tall behind them. It was a gorgeous building, but Molly and Theo were focused on the horizon to the east. The sky was getting lighter, a pale azure blue tinged with pink and orange as the golden orb of the sun began to glow on the edge of the ocean.

Theo moved to stand behind Molly and wrapped his arms around her waist, resting his chin on the top of her head and inhaling the orange perfume of her hair. They stood in silence, mesmerised by the colours of nature, waiting to be among the first people to see the sun rise in Australia on this day.

Seagulls and cormorants wheeled in the sky above their heads and the tang of the sea carried to them on the warm breeze. Theo breathed deeply, taking time to feel the moment, committing it to memory. He knew this experience would stay with him always, long after he'd returned to his life in Sydney.

'This is incredible,' he told Molly. 'Thank you for bringing me here.' He had been brought up to be busy, to be achieving, and found he was always thinking about something. He was comfortable here in Byron Bay. With Molly in his arms. He felt at home. He knew he had a job to do but he still had time and space to breathe. It was a rare state for him. 'It's not often I feel completely at peace,' he added.

'What are the things that bring you peace?' Molly asked.

He could count those things on one hand. 'Playing the guitar—not performing, but playing on my own with no one to hear. It's cathartic and freeing. Watching the sunrise at the Temple of Borobudur in Indonesia—that was a very similar experience to today.' And being with Molly.

But he didn't include that last one, knowing it would be very likely to frighten her. They weren't at a point where they had serious conversations. He knew they might never be. That she might never want that.

The sun was well and truly above the horizon now. The rich pinks and oranges had faded, leaving just a cloudless blue sky and a new day.

'But every day is a new beginning. A chance to start again. What are your plans for your new future? Where do you see yourself in five years?' He tried to gently gauge her thoughts.

'Five years!' Molly exclaimed. 'I haven't really thought about it. Have you?'

'I might be running the clinics by then.'

'Is that what you want?'

'It's what's expected,' he replied. 'I've imagined other options plenty of times, but I've never seriously considered doing anything else. Maybe I should just stay here,' he said, and he was only half joking.

The sun was on Molly's face. She was glowing. Her hair was like spun gold and her eyes were the colour of the sky. She looked like an angel and he knew there was nowhere else he'd rather be.

He studied her closely, committing the vision

to memory, knowing he would take that image with him when he left.

Molly couldn't believe another week had passed. The year was rapidly drawing to a close, Christmas was three weeks away and Theo was over halfway through his stint in Byron Bay. She had to admit that she was enjoying spending time with him. She'd relaxed, realised her friends were happy for her and no one was judging her. She was free to do as she pleased. Theo gave her the space she needed and was happy to see her on her terms. It had been a fun few weeks.

The weekends had passed by in a blur of sun, the sea, sand and sex—not always in that order—and the weekdays had been filled with work and the myriad social activities that were part of the fabric of daily life in Byron. The days were busy and so were the nights.

It was Friday again and Molly and Theo were the last ones at the office. Theo's consulting room door was open when Molly went to see if he was ready to leave. It was Gemma's birthday and they were meeting friends at the Railway Hotel for an open mic night. Theo was on the phone but motioned for Molly to come in.

'I've got a few ideas. I'll talk to you again once I've got more information,' Theo said as he ended the call, but not before Molly worked out he was on the phone to his mother and they were talking about the clinic.

'Is everything okay?' she asked.

Theo nodded and switched off his computer before standing up. 'Mum just had a few questions about the clinic.'

Molly looked expectantly at Theo, waiting for him to expand.

He pushed his chair under the desk and Molly waited. 'The clinic's profits are down and she wants my opinion on a couple of things,' he said.

'What sort of things?'

'She's looked at the books but while that gives her the bottom line it doesn't indicate the reason why the figures have dropped. She wants to know what I can tell her.'

'She wants you to spy on us?'

'No.' Theo frowned. 'Why would you think that?'

'Because you were talking about getting information.'

'Why do you always think the worst of me?'

'What do you mean?'

'You accused me of keeping my relationship with the boss, my mother, a secret, when really it just wasn't relevant.'

'But it is relevant now, isn't it?' Molly argued.

'You wouldn't be reporting back to her about profits if you weren't her son.'

'This has nothing to do with the fact we're related and now you're accusing me of being a spy.'

'All those questions you were asking Matt about the hydrotherapy sessions—you were looking for information for your mother, weren't you?' Those questions that had seemed so random now made sense.

'Yes, but I'm not spying on *you* or any of the staff. I'm looking at the figures, at the way the clinic operates.'

'Does anyone else know what you're doing?'

He nodded. 'Tom was aware and Paula has been helping me with the data. I've been looking at where we can make money or save money, if there's a service we should be offering or one that isn't viable. It's not so much a staffing issue as a practice management one. I haven't been hiding this, Molly. Why don't you trust me?'

Molly thought about Theo's question. He was right, she was always questioning his behaviour, looking for reasons to push him away. 'You know trust is an issue for me. People I've cared about have let me down. A lot.'

'Have I let you down in any way?'

Molly shook her head. 'Not yet.'

'Why do you assume I'm going to?'

'Because men I care about seem to,' she admitted. 'My father. Daniel. People lie to me, people cheat and I've been gullible before, believing things I know I shouldn't, and not trusting my instincts.'

'I'm not keeping secrets from you,' he said. 'This is simply an admin issue, part and parcel of running the business. If there's anything that affects you, I'll tell you,' he added as he wrapped an arm around her shoulders and dropped a kiss on her forehead. Her hurt feelings gave way to guilt. She'd made this about her. She expected to be let down, but he hadn't done anything to her. She knew he was under no obligation to tell her about what he was doing. She wouldn't have expected Tom to tell her anything in the same situation. Theo didn't owe her an explanation just because they were sleeping together. They weren't in a serious relationship. That was her choice. She couldn't have her cake and eat it too.

'I'm sorry—again,' she apologised.

He dropped a kiss on her lips before releasing her from his embrace. 'It's okay, just remember we're on the same side,' he said as he went to the cupboard in the corner of his consulting room and retrieved his guitar.

* * *

Theo forced himself to join in Gemma's birthday festivities and leave Molly's comments for another time. But he couldn't deny her comments had upset him. Why did it always seem to be two steps forwards and one back, or maybe even one forwards and two backwards with her? She was so afraid of letting him close. He understood that she was fearful and he agreed, trust needed to be earned, but it hurt when he knew he'd done nothing to make her think she couldn't trust him. It made it difficult to prove that he was trustworthy when she was inclined to make assumptions. Inclined to tar him with the same brush as her father and Daniel.

It shouldn't matter. Their relationship wasn't serious. But he didn't want Molly to confuse him with other men in her life.

He took his guitar out of its case and began to tune it. Strumming the strings calmed him down and he was able to take some comfort in the fact that Molly had admitted she cared about him. But how much was what he wanted to know.

'Are you going to sing, Theo?' Gemma asked.

'I'm not sure,' he replied. He didn't know if he was in the right mood to sing in front of people tonight.

'These sessions are popular so you should put

your name down. You can always decline later,' Matt said. 'I reckon we'd all be keen to hear a new voice. The talent can be a bit hit and miss.'

Encouraged by their group, he signed up to sing, and when he returned to the table Gemma said, 'Molly told me you worked overseas. Can I pick your brains?'

'Sure. Did she tell you I worked with an aid organisation so we were clinic-based, not hospital-based? Is that what you're thinking of doing?'

Gemma nodded. 'I think I'd like that. Where did you go?'

'I spent two years in Cambodia and Indonesia.'

'You'd recommend it?'

Theo nodded. 'It was one of the most amazing experiences of my life.' He had loved the freedom of being away from the expectations of his parents. There were other expectations but they were manageable, he wasn't expected to be better than anyone else, he was only expected to be as good, and that had felt liberating. 'It was challenging a lot of the time, but knowing that we were actually making a difference was unbelievably rewarding. Everyone should be entitled to health care. It's a basic human right, not a privilege, and to be able to deliver that to people was incredible.'

'Why did you come back?'

'My parents expected me to go into their business.'

'What's that?'

'The clinic.'

'Pacific Coast?'

Theo nodded. 'Lian Chin is my mother,' he told them. 'My parents set up the clinic and my mother runs it.' He figured there was no point in keeping his relationship hidden. They'd find out eventually.

'That must make things hard for you at times,' Gemma said.

'It has its ups and downs,' he admitted.

He was aware of Molly watching him. She'd been quiet since they got to the pub and he wished he knew what she was thinking. Did she still think that he was hiding something from her? Or did she think, after his conversation with his mother, that he thought medicine was all about the money? That wasn't his mindset. After working overseas he knew that money was much less important than helping people. But that didn't mean it wasn't important at all.

He strummed a few chords on his guitar and, using the cover of his music to keep the others from overhearing, he said to Molly, 'Everything okay?' He wasn't going to sit there and second-guess what she was thinking.

She smiled and nodded. Her smile reached her eyes and Theo relaxed. Perhaps she wasn't upset with him at all, he thought as he was called up to the stage.

He debated whether or not to sing a love song to Molly before thinking better of it. He didn't want to embarrass Molly or himself. She might have said everything was okay, but that didn't mean she was ready to listen to him sing her a love song in public. A Christmas song was another option. Christmas was fast approaching and the streets and businesses had their decorations on display, but the audience possibly wasn't the right demographic for Christmas carols. An Aussie rock classic might be a better choice.

The crowd loved his rendition and demanded a second song as he wrapped it up. Molly was smiling and clapping along with the rest of the crowd. He'd do it for her.

'If you recognise this one, sing the chorus with me,' he invited as he launched into 'I Still Call Australia Home'.

This song had a slow beginning and as he kept his gaze on Molly and sang he reflected on how comfortable he felt in Byron Bay. He was reminded of the freedom he'd had when he'd worked overseas, where he was expected to do his job but no more or less than the other doctors working with him. Here was the same. Here he was just Theo. Not the boss's son, despite what Molly might think. Here he was just Theo, especially when he was with Molly. Then he forgot about anything else.

Molly was still smiling when he finished the next song and she welcomed him off stage with a kiss and, suddenly, all was right in his world again.

At midday on Monday Molly knocked on Theo's door and invited him to lunch in the staffroom.

'What's the occasion? Another birthday?' Theo asked.

Molly shook her head. 'No. I hope you don't mind but I asked everyone to spend some time thinking about what is working in the practice and what isn't. I thought they might have some suggestions or opinions that you haven't thought of and that you could add to your report.'

Molly was trying to make up for what she thought of as her unkindness, the accusations she'd made about Theo last Friday. He had tried to help her four years ago and she hadn't listened. He needed help now and it was her turn to listen. She wanted to help.

'You did? Why?'

Oh, God, had she got it wrong? He hadn't wanted her help at all.

'I thought it was my chance to help you. A way of saying sorry for all the times I've misjudged you.'

'Thank you.' Theo smiled and gave her a quick kiss on her cheek and Molly breathed a sigh of relief that he wasn't annoyed with her for interfering. 'Let's go.'

Paula, Matt and Gemma were already seated around the table, buzzing with ideas. Molly knew Theo had already got data from Paula, and a few suggestions regarding administrative issues, but she also knew Paula was keen to be involved further.

'Okay, let's start with what's working well.' Molly got the ball rolling.

'Our consulting lists are consistently around ninety per cent booked. For both the physios and GPs.'

'Do you think we have enough staff. Is there need for more?' Theo asked.

'We've got room for more but I don't think the demand is there. Summer is a bit busier but winter is steady also,' Paula replied.

'I think we could get more use out of the pool if we had more staff,' Matt added. 'An extra physio might let us maximise its potential in terms of rehab, but alternatively we might be able to rent it out for swimming lessons or aquarobics, as we talked about, Theo. It's an expensive asset so it would be good to get more income from it.'

'Paula, you said we have room for more staff. If we don't need more GPs or treating physiotherapists, what are some options for the vacant consulting rooms? And why are they vacant?' Theo wanted to know.

'The consulting rooms that are available to be booked by visiting specialists aren't being used as often because the new hospital is finished and they're going there instead,' Paula said.

'Who else would be willing to take on a permanent lease of some of this space?' Theo looked up from his note-taking to look around the group assembled at the table.

'I think allied health staff could be a good value add to the clinic. A podiatrist, a dietician, a psychologist. Someone like that might be interested in renting space on a permanent basis. Even a dentist is an option,' Molly said.

'Or we could open up those offices and make better use of the space,' Matt suggested.

'As what?'

'We could combine spaces to make a Pilates

or yoga studio. I don't think that would be hard to do. The building has been added onto over the years and doesn't present as a new modern space and doesn't work as well as it could,' he answered.

Theo was taking notes. 'All good points, thank you. There's one final issue that I think is worth raising,' he said. 'Are we billing efficiently and adequately?' He directed his attention to Paula before turning his gaze to the others around the table. 'Paula has given me access to the books and I realise this query is only a small component, but every little bit saved or earned may make a difference.'

'What do you mean?' Paula asked.

'On my first day here, Molly and I treated a walk-in patient, the gentleman who went into cardiac arrest.' Theo waited for Paula's confirmation nod before continuing. 'The reception staff told me afterwards that he was only charged the government fee for that service. Not a regular consulting fee. Why was that?'

'It's what we've always done for emergency consults,' Paula explained.

'But we're not an emergency department.'

'They wouldn't have been charged if they'd turned up at the public hospital emergency department.'

'But we're not a public hospital either,' Theo replied. 'And private hospital emergency clinics charge hundreds of dollars to treat patients. We should too. We're not a public service. We should be charging full fees.'

'Emergency presentations can be quite stressful and it seems mercenary in those times to be talking about money,' Paula responded.

'I get that, believe me,' Theo replied. 'But if people are frequently using the clinic as their emergency department instead of going to the hospital, then if they have the means to pay for our service, they should be charged.'

'What about your comment last Friday? You said everyone should have access to health care as a basic right.' Molly felt she had to ask the question.

Theo nodded. 'That is my opinion and in Australia the government provides free or subsidised health care to people who need it. But Pacific Coast Clinics is a business—it needs to make a profit. We are not funded by the government and we should expect people to pay if they are able to and be prepared to have a conversation about finances if the need arises. If the reception staff don't feel comfortable doing that, is that something you could take on, Paula?'

Paula nodded as Theo wrapped up the meeting. 'Thank you, everyone, and thank you, Molly, for instigating the meeting. I should have asked you all for your opinions earlier but I'm used to operating on my own, but I appreciate your input.'

Molly tugged on her dress as she stepped out of the car. She'd bought a new outfit in celebration of the staff Christmas function, a sleeveless shirt dress that buttoned down the front, but it felt a little tighter today than she recalled it being when she'd purchased it. Perhaps she and Theo had been out for too many meals, she thought as she undid a couple of buttons at the bottom to give her room to bend her knees—the Christmas function was barefoot bowls and she needed to be able to squat to play. She'd just have to live with the button at her waist that was a bit snug.

'Who would like a glass of bubbly?' Matt greeted Molly, Theo and Gemma on arrival. He had an open bottle in one hand and several glasses in the other.

Molly took a glass and held it as Matt poured for her. She wasn't going back to Sydney for Christmas with her family this year, she had volunteered to work between Christmas and New Year so the other doctors could take holidays, so tonight was going to be one of her main celebrations, but as she brought the glass to her lips a wave of nausea washed over her. She felt light-headed. She wondered if it was something to do with her dress being a little tight at the waist or maybe she was just dehydrated. She was feeling a little hot.

She put the glass down on a nearby table and decided to start with a water. The water helped briefly. Until the finger food was passed around. Smoked salmon, chicken sandwiches, marinated prawns, all of it made her stomach turn.

Molly tried distracting herself by joining in an end of bowls, but all the bending made her dizzy. Eventually she gave up and went home, insisting that Theo stay and enjoy the evening, and just assuming she'd picked up a virus from somewhere.

She was lethargic and felt less than one hundred per cent for the next couple of days with bouts of light-headedness but no vomiting and no temperature. She'd lost her appetite, with the exception of Vegemite toast, and reluctantly took Monday off work.

By Monday afternoon, she was feeling better, provided she wasn't looking at food and didn't stand up too quickly.

'Did you have a terribly busy day because of me?' she asked Gemma when she got home, feeling guilty because she knew her patients had either had their appointments cancelled or had been moved to Gemma's or Theo's lists.

'No, it was all fine,' Gemma replied. 'Theo says hi.'

She had told Theo to stay away but he'd phoned and messaged her during the day. There was no point in passing a virus around to more people. And in her mind a summer romance didn't include nursing care.

'I brought you something,' Gemma said as she handed Molly a bag.

Molly peered inside and her eyes widened when she saw the contents. 'What's this for?' she asked as she withdrew a box containing a pregnancy test kit.

'Just a precaution. You have to admit your symptoms fit this cause.'

'Don't be ridiculous,' Molly argued as she quickly calculated the time since she and Theo had had unprotected sex.

'When was your last period?' Gemma asked.

Molly couldn't recall. She remembered the lack of contraception two and a half weeks ago. The morning-after pill. Gemma didn't know about any of that. But was her period late? Maybe a few days late, although she couldn't be sure.

'There's no harm in doing a test,' Gemma said, and Molly gave in, knowing Gemma was unlikely to let the matter drop.

She felt the nausea return as she went to the bathroom and did the test. She left the little stick on the toilet seat, washed her hands and went back to the kitchen to put the kettle on. She needed to distract herself.

'Are you going to check it or am I?' Gemma asked as they finished the tea Molly made.

Molly wasn't sure she was game but said, 'I'll do it.' After all, it was her issue.

She returned to the bathroom. The stick was where she'd left it, looking innocent enough, until she got closer.

Two pink lines greeted her.

Molly picked up the stick before sitting down on the toilet lid. She closed her eyes and concentrated on breathing.

She heard the bathroom door open and looked up to find Gemma standing in the doorway, her eyes fixed on the stick that was still in Molly's hand.

'It's positive?' she said.

Molly nodded before promptly bursting into tears. Gemma stepped forward and wrapped her in a hug.

‘Should I do another test? It might be wrong,’ Molly said, her voice full of hope.

‘A false negative maybe,’ Gemma replied, ‘but a false positive is unlikely.’

Molly knew Gemma was right. ‘What am I going to do?’ she asked.

‘Nothing right now,’ was Gemma’s reply. ‘I’m going to make you a piece of toast and another cup of tea. You’ll eat and drink and take a breath. Take a minute.’

‘This is not part of my plan.’ Did she have a plan? She didn’t really. Her plan had been to spend some time focusing on herself.

*I should never have got involved with Theo*, she thought, but she wasn’t sure she really meant it.

She’d enjoyed spending time with him. Sleeping with him. Until now.

‘What do I tell Theo?’ she asked Gemma. ‘We agreed on a summer romance, a “friends with benefits” type scenario. I don’t think a baby counts as a benefit,’ Molly said.

‘Some people might think it does,’ Gemma suggested.

Molly shook her head. ‘No. We didn’t plan on this. I didn’t plan on this.’ She’d told Theo as much.

‘No kidding.’ Gemma wrapped her arm around

Molly and helped her to her feet. 'Come with me, I'll put the kettle on.'

Molly collapsed onto a stool at the kitchen bench. '*Do* I tell Theo?'

'Why wouldn't you?'

'Our relationship is hardly serious. And I don't want to be tied to a man because of a mistake. I don't want to be tied to a man at all. The next relationship I'm in will be by choice, not circumstance.'

'In that case you only have one option because you can't, in all honesty, keep the baby and not tell Theo.'

'There is another option,' she said. 'Theo might not want anything to do with me or the baby.'

'But that would still mean telling him and taking that chance. Do you honestly think he wouldn't choose you and the baby?'

Molly didn't know what to think but she did know she couldn't terminate a pregnancy. She was filled with despair as she realised that a brief lapse of concentration was going to change her life. She hadn't planned on having children, but she knew she would struggle with a termination.

And that was the second time Gemma had used the word honest. Molly knew she was right. She had to be honest. She had to tell Theo.

It was only seventeen days ago that she'd told Theo she didn't want children. Could she do this? Could she raise a child? Could she do it alone?

Molly's hands were sweaty. She thought she might throw up but she knew tonight's nausea wasn't related to her pregnancy hormones, but to nerves. More than nerves. It was triggered by fear. She was going to tell Theo her news, their news, and she was terrified.

He might want nothing to do with her or the baby or he might want to be involved. Both options had pros and cons. Both options were equally terrifying. One would mean she would lose her independence. She would have to accommodate Theo in her plans and she'd be permanently tied to him through their child. They would be permanently connected and she did *not* want to be tied to a man out of obligation.

The other option would mean she would lose Theo. She was prepared to be a single mother but was that fair on a child?

Now that she was between a rock and a hard place she found that things were not so black and white. It was a lot more complicated in real life. Theory and practice were two very different things and she really had no idea how she wanted this to play out.

She'd have to put the ball in Theo's court and go from there.

She checked the time. She had ten minutes before Theo would arrive. She'd invited him for dinner. She had managed to avoid him at work—she knew she wouldn't be able to pretend everything was fine and the issue was not one she could discuss at work. Dinner was the best, the only, option and thankfully Gemma had agreed to make herself scarce for the evening and leave the apartment free for Molly and Theo.

Molly found a playlist on her phone and connected it to the speakers, using the music to settle her nerves. She lit the mosquito coils and placed one under the table and the other near the herb pots in the corner of the balcony. She finished setting the table and filled a jug with cold water. Bustling around kept her hands busy and her mind occupied.

Before leaving the house, Gemma had made a chicken salad for Molly to serve for dinner. Molly couldn't face the thought of cooking and the idea of handling raw meat brought on another bout of nausea. If it wasn't for Gemma's help Molly would be serving toast with Vegemite—

that was about all she could manage to prepare at present.

She switched on the fairy lights that were strung around the balcony and then turned on the Christmas tree lights. Gemma had decorated the house for Christmas, which was now only two weeks away.

Molly would have the apartment to herself over Christmas. Gemma was going to Brisbane but, as Molly had volunteered to work between Christmas and New Year, Matt and Levi had invited her to have Christmas dinner with them, and she was happy to have a reason not to go to Sydney. She would miss her sisters but she wasn't ready to leave Byron Bay yet. She had found some inner peace since moving here—although her peace had been shattered a little with the events of the past week—but that was another good reason to stay away from Sydney. She needed some time to work out how to announce the situation to her family. To work out how to tell them they would be grandparents and aunts.

She wasn't sure how that news would be received. She thought her sisters would be excited; she hoped her mother would be too, but there was no way of knowing. Her mother had learnt to guard her emotions a long time ago.

Molly wondered what Theo did for Christmas. He would be back in Sydney by then.

She wondered what his family would think of her news. Would he tell them?

Her musings were cut short by a knock on the door. Her heart skipped a beat when she opened it. Even though she knew it would be Theo the sight of him still took her breath away. He looked good.

He was wearing a pair of pale cotton shorts and a black T-shirt. His face was tanned and he looked healthy and strong and gorgeous. Molly knew he'd enjoyed his time in Byron and she was about to make sure it was time he'd never forget. One way or the other.

He kissed her and she closed her eyes and let herself imagine, just for a moment, a future where she could trust him not to break her heart. A future where they could be happy.

But any future they would have was now going to be complicated by her pregnancy. Things were never going to be the same. Never going to be simple.

As Theo released her she was overcome by a wave of light-headedness. 'There's beer in the fridge or water on the table. Help yourself to a drink. I'll be back in a minute,' she said as she fled to the bathroom.

She splashed her face with cold water and took two deep breaths before drying her face. She applied concealer to cover up the dark circles under her eyes and then rejoined Theo for a dinner that she couldn't face eating.

Gemma's chicken salad was delicious but Molly's appetite was non-existent. She picked at her dinner, moving food around her plate, while she tried to make conversation.

'Are you sure you're feeling better?' Theo asked. 'You're very quiet and you've barely touched your meal.'

'There's something I need to tell you,' Molly said as she put her knife and fork together on her plate and pushed it aside. She could feel her dinner pressing against her oesophagus, threatening to make a reappearance. Theo was watching her closely, waiting. She almost felt sorry for him, he had no idea what was coming, but this was as much his fault as hers. He needed to hear what she had to say. 'I didn't have a virus. I assumed that I'd caught something but it turns out that wasn't the case.' She glanced away as she summoned up her courage before returning her gaze to Theo. 'I'm pregnant.'

Theo was silent. Molly waited, willing him to speak but at the same time dreading what he might say.

'Pregnant? Not sick?'

Molly shook her head. 'Obviously I'm one of those statistics you read about in the pamphlet that comes with the morning-after pill.' She must have ovulated before they had sex. 'Our timing wasn't great.'

'Pregnant. Wow.' A smile slowly spread across his face.

Molly frowned. 'You're not upset?'

'Upset? No. This is amazing,' he said as he stood and moved around the table, taking her hands in his and pulling her to her feet. 'We're having a baby.'

He wrapped her in a hug and kissed her and for a minute, Molly forgot that she was planning on doing this alone. This was not the reaction she'd anticipated and it felt good to share this moment with Theo. But that wasn't going to be her reality.

'How is this good news?' she asked.

'I've always wanted to be a father and I think, I hope, I'll be a good one. I've had plenty of lessons in how not to raise a family,' he said, but he must have heard something in her voice because he stepped back, releasing her, and looked into her eyes. 'You're not happy about this? I know you said you didn't want children…'

She heard the note of hope in his voice and

knew he was counting on her changing her mind. 'I'm keeping it,' she told him, giving him the news she knew he wanted, 'but we didn't plan on having a baby. We barely know each other.'

'There are worse things that have happened. We're not the first ones to find ourselves in this situation. We can make it work.'

'Make what work?'

'Us.'

Molly shook her head and sat down. She needed a bit of space, physically and mentally. 'There is no us, Theo. We had no plans past the next two weeks.'

'We'll make plans.'

He made it sound so simple. But Molly knew it was far from that. Unexpected tears welled in her eyes and she blinked quickly, trying to stop them from spilling over. 'Neither of us signed up for parenthood.'

'That doesn't mean we can't do this.'

'Theo, we agreed to a summer romance. We didn't agree to raising a baby.'

'What do you suggest we do, then?'

This was moving faster than Molly had anticipated. She'd barely accepted the fact she was pregnant and she hadn't expected to start making plans tonight. 'I don't know. I'm still trying to work out how this happened.' She felt sick.

'Shall I tell you what I'm thinking?'

Molly nodded. There could be no harm in hearing Theo's thoughts. Unless he wanted to take the baby and raise it on his own. Despite not having motherhood in her future plans a week ago, Molly knew now she couldn't give her child up.

'What if you came back to Sydney with me? What if we got married?'

# CHAPTER NINE

'WHAT?'

*He wanted to get married?*

Molly shook her head.

*That was a ridiculous idea.*

Unexpected and ridiculous.

'I have no plans to move to Sydney and I don't want to get married.'

'Why not?' he asked.

'We agreed to a summer romance. We hadn't talked about anything after that and suddenly you're talking about spending the rest of our lives together.' Molly paused to take a breath, she could hear a slightly panicked note creeping into her voice and she needed to calm down. 'That makes no sense. I don't want to be trapped in a marriage because of a baby. And I don't think you do either.'

'Would you prefer I went back to Sydney and left you to it?' he asked. 'That's not going to happen. I barely saw my mother and father growing up. You know I was basically raised by my grandparents. I want to be present for my child. I want to be involved.'

'I'm not saying you can't be involved.'

'Maybe not, but you are saying you're happy to have a summer romance but you don't want a relationship. You'll have my baby, but you don't want to marry me.'

'I don't want to marry anyone.'

'But I'm not just anyone,' he argued. 'I'm the father of your child. I don't want to be cut out of my child's life. If we're married that can't happen.'

'I'm not trying to cut you out.'

'But you want to make all the decisions.'

'Not all,' Molly replied, 'but I do want to be able to make some. Starting with whether or not to get married. I don't want to be told what to do, how to think, where to live.'

'I wasn't,' Theo objected.

'You just did! Literally three minutes after I told you the news you said, let's move to Sydney. Let's get married. As if I don't get a say.'

'Of course, you get a say, but would it be so awful to do this together?'

No, it wouldn't. In her heart she could see the future. But she couldn't risk it. The future wouldn't turn out as she hoped—she'd learnt that much. Happily ever after only existed in fairy tales.

Molly wiped away a tear. Theo had proposed out of honour. He hadn't proposed because he was in love with her. He hadn't proposed of his own accord. He'd proposed because of the circumstances, because he thought it was the *right* thing to do, and she couldn't accept. She would *not* end up like her mother—trapped in a marriage with a man who didn't love her.

'I don't want to lose my independence. My mother was hamstrung by her circumstances. She had no career and no money. I've worked hard to make sure I have financial independence. What I didn't always have was emotional independence. I was too busy seeking validation. Now I have both and I'm not prepared to give them up.'

'Commitment and dependence are not the same thing.'

Molly shook her head. Theo was wrong. 'I spent years being Daniel's girlfriend, Daniel's on-again-off-again girlfriend. The girl Daniel cheated on. Now I'm going to be someone's mother. I don't want to be someone's wife. I want to be me. Molly.'

'You will always be Molly. I'm not trying to change you. I'm trying to support you.'

But Molly was worried that support might end up feeling like control. She needed to breathe. She needed some space. 'We're not going to sort this out tonight.'

'I agree,' Theo said. 'We should sleep on it and talk tomorrow. But,' he said as he kissed her goodnight, 'I want you to remember this is good news and we will work it out.'

Molly collapsed on her bed after Theo left. She knew she should clean up but she was exhausted. Emotionally and physically.

Theo wanted to marry her.

For a brief mad moment she'd been tempted to say yes.

But he didn't love her. He just wanted to make sure he saw his child.

It was ludicrous to think that their story could end in marriage. In happily ever after.

She was having a baby; she was going to be a mother. She was going to co-parent with Theo. That was enough commitment for now.

Marriage was unnecessary.

And marriage without love was ridiculous.

'So, you'll let me know the date of your first ultrasound scan?' Theo confirmed as he signalled for their dinner bill. Just the thought of that first scan, of seeing his baby's heart beating on a screen for the first time, filled Theo with joy, a sense of anticipation and happiness more intense than anything he could have imagined.

'You'll come up from Sydney for it?' Molly asked and Theo nodded. 'How will you manage that?'

'I'll make it work. I'll take annual leave days. As long as you give me enough notice I can block out my diary.'

He was due to return to Sydney on Tuesday, in three days' time. His six-week stint was coming to an end and he still hadn't convinced Molly to move with him, but he had no intention of missing those milestones. He needed to show Molly he was serious about being involved and that started with the antenatal appointments. He hadn't figured out yet how he'd manage to attend antenatal classes—he assumed Molly would be going—but there was time for that. He knew there was a fine line to tread between being interested, being involved and Molly thinking he was trying to control her pregnancy. Her life.

He was so grateful that Molly had chosen to keep the baby and he was going to do everything in his power to support her, as well as make sure he was involved in the pregnancy and beyond. The huge responsibility of raising a child wasn't lost on him but it was a duty he would embrace.

He would prefer to do it side by side with Molly, as partners, not co-parents, but that outcome was still a work in progress. Molly had taken it off the table but Theo wasn't giving up yet.

He'd invited Molly to dinner and they'd spent the night talking about logistics, which was important and necessary, but Theo knew there was also plenty being left unsaid. There was no discussion about how they felt. The conversation had been practical, not emotional.

Perhaps he should have cooked for her at home. In the privacy of his house maybe they would have been more honest with each other, more forthcoming about their feelings, their hopes and dreams. Perhaps he'd suggest that for tomorrow night.

He knew he was running out of time. He knew that once he moved to Sydney it would be harder to convince Molly that they should be together. He was worried it would be out of sight, out of mind. That was another reason he was determined to travel to Byron Bay for appointments. He wanted to remain in Molly's life.

Four days after hearing Molly's news he was still overcome with emotion, excitement and nervousness. It was exhilarating but terrifying all at the same time. He was determined to be a good father, a loving father, a hands-on father—all the things he'd missed out on—but working out how to make this happen was going to be a challenge.

He'd briefly considered staying in Byron Bay but he knew that ultimately he couldn't run the family business from there and that was what was expected of him, what he expected of himself. There were three clinics in Sydney—that was where he needed to be. It was frustrating but he'd figure out a solution eventually. He was not going to be an absent father. He could see a future with Molly. He just had to figure out how to convince her.

Trust was the key.

He needed time to show her that she could depend on him.

He hadn't suggested marriage again. He knew he'd got that wrong. She'd said she wouldn't marry him. He should take comfort from the fact she'd said she wouldn't marry anyone. But he wasn't just anyone. He was the father of her child.

'So, we agree, open lines of communication are important,' he said as he paid the bill. 'We will make this work. We both want to do what's best for our child. I'm sure all parents think they'll do things differently but I really want to get this right.'

'I do—' Molly's reply was interrupted by the

sound of screeching tyres as a car rounded the corner outside the restaurant at speed. The noise level in the restaurant dropped as conversation among all the diners ceased when they heard a deafening crash and the unmistakeable sound of metal crunching and glass shattering.

There was a brief moment of absolute silence before a car horn blared and continued incessantly. Overlaying that came the sound of a second crash, duller than the first, followed by screaming.

Theo and Molly ran out to the street. A cloud of dust billowed in the air, choking the intersection.

Theo sprinted down the road, heading towards the screams and the dust, and Molly dashed after him. She rounded the corner and came to a stop, giving her brain a moment to process what she was seeing.

A car had careened up onto the footpath and was jammed between two concrete planter boxes, its nose against the wall of an old two-storey building that operated as a wine bar.

Molly knew the wine bar had an outdoor dining area on the street, under the veranda. The planter pots were supposed to act as a barrier, as protection for the outside tables, but somehow the car had flipped onto its side and slid in between the planter pots, taking out a veranda post in the process. The veranda had collapsed and she could see broken chairs and tables lying crushed under the weight of the veranda. She had to assume that, moments before, people had been sitting at those tables.

It was a confronting scene. Debris was strewn across the road as the dust began to settle and Molly's heart was in her throat at the thought of what carnage might be revealed. They needed to find out if there were people trapped under the building.

People were milling around—dazed and stunned—and Molly saw some crawling out from under the veranda. Bystanders helped them to their feet. Others had phones to their ears and Molly could hear them talking to emergency services. The police station wasn't far away and she expected they would be on the scene quickly.

She looked for Theo. They should start tending to the injured victims.

She found him clambering up onto one of the concrete planter pots to peer into the driver's car window. The window was cracked and he punched it, knocking it in, before reaching his hand inside.

Molly peered through the rear window of the

car. She could see the driver slumped over the wheel. He was covered in white powder from the airbag, bleeding from the head. Theo was feeling for a pulse. She couldn't see a passenger on the other side of the car. That didn't mean there wasn't one, but the car was jammed tight between the planter pots and the building. There was no way of opening a door. No way of getting to anyone inside.

Theo climbed down from the car. 'He's alive but unconscious,' he said as they heard sirens in the distance.

'Could you see anyone else in the car?' Molly asked.

Theo shook his head as a young man emerged from the rubble at their feet. Theo grabbed him under his armpits and helped him stand. He was covered in blood and dust.

'You have to help me. My girlfriend is in there,' he said, pointing back under the building. 'She's trapped under the car.'

Molly saw Theo's quick glance in the direction of the car. 'Is she conscious? Breathing?' he asked.

Molly knew he was really asking if the girl was alive.

'I don't know.' Tears spilt from the man's eyes,

making muddy streaks through the dirt on his face. 'Her leg is trapped; I can't get her out.'

'What's her name?' Theo asked as Molly put a hand on the man's arm, offering comfort through touch but feeling that was all too inadequate given the circumstances.

'Bree.'

Theo dropped to his knees and before Molly could ask what he was doing he had crawled under the car and into the rubble.

Molly's eyes widened. What on earth was he doing?

The veranda posts creaked and groaned and dropped another couple of inches.

What was he thinking? He was putting himself in danger. For what? What did he think he would be able to do? He couldn't move the car.

Her heart was in her throat as she sent up a silent plea in the hope someone or something was listening.

*God, please let him be okay. Get him out before he gets hurt. Before anything else goes wrong.*

She rested her right hand on her stomach, subconsciously shielding her baby from harm. She knew it was a reflex action, instinctive, protective. She knew her baby was okay, but her baby's father was a different matter.

Staring at the black hole into which Theo had disappeared, she knew she'd made a mistake. She'd been an idiot. So fixated on maintaining her independence, her control, that she was risking everything.

She wanted Theo in her life. She *needed* him in her life. Not just for their child's sake. But for hers.

Molly was quite prepared to be a single mother. She had no issue with raising a child on her own or making independent decisions but, confronted with the reality of the danger Theo had put himself in, she realised her plan had a few flaws. She was quite prepared to raise a child as a single mother, but she wasn't prepared for her child not to have a father at all.

Now that Theo was in danger, she realised she didn't want to think of a world without him.

She didn't want to live without him. He made her happy. He made her a better person and she liked who she was when she was with him. Why was she refusing to accept that? Why was she resisting taking a chance on a serious relationship?

She admitted it would be difficult if he was in Sydney. *She'd* made this difficult. Not impossible, but not as easy as it could have been.

What if he was right? What if she could have commitment and independence? What if she could have a relationship with him without losing her identity? Without losing control?

It had to be worth a try.

She made a promise to herself. If, when, he came back to her they would have a conversation. They would make a new plan. She would tell him how she felt.

And if she lost him?

She shook her head to clear her thoughts. She couldn't think about that now. She needed something else to think about. Something other than Theo and the danger he'd put himself in. She turned to the young man who still stood beside her. She would let him distract her from her worries about Theo.

He was pale, his eyes were wide and he was starting to shake. He was in shock.

Molly turned to one of the bystanders. 'We need a blanket,' she said. 'Can you see if any of the restaurants have something we could borrow?'

The street was full of bars and restaurants and most had outdoor seating. Molly knew they would have blankets to ward off the chill on the odd cool night.

She turned back to the young man. 'What's your name?' she asked.

'Josh.'

'Josh, my name is Molly. I'm a doctor. I think you should sit down.' She guided him away from the crash site, not far away, just away from the damaged veranda. She didn't want to put him at risk if there was a further collapse. She got him to sit on the edge of the footpath with his feet in the gutter and wrapped the blanket around his shoulders when someone brought it to her.

'Are you hurt?' she asked as she sat beside him. He didn't appear to have sustained any major injuries. She could see a few abrasions and he had blood on his hands, but she wasn't sure whose blood it was.

He shook his head. 'But Bree—' His voice cracked and he couldn't finish his sentence.

'My friend who's gone to Bree, he's a doctor as well,' Molly told him, hoping that gave him some reassurance. She had to raise her voice as the emergency vehicles turned into the street with their sirens blaring. As the police cars, fire engines and ambulances pulled to a stop the sirens were switched off, but their flashing red and blue lights lent an eerie air to the scene.

Molly stood up to introduce herself as a policewoman approached.

'Do you need assistance?' the policewoman asked.

'No. Josh's injuries are minor, and the driver

of the car was alive immediately after the accident, but my colleague—' Her voice caught as she thought about Theo. 'My colleague couldn't get to him so we don't know the extent of his injuries. We think he was alone in the car but we're not certain.'

'Where is your colleague?'

Molly pointed at the car. 'He's gone in there. There's a young woman, this man's girlfriend, trapped under the car. We don't know if there are any others.' She could see other people with bloodied heads, bloodied hands and torn and dirty clothes, but she didn't know if there were any others unaccounted for.

The policewoman nodded. 'Okay, thanks for the information.'

As she turned to leave, Molly stopped her. 'Can you take Josh to the paramedics? He's in shock and needs someone to keep an eye on him. I need to wait here.' Molly could have done it, but she wasn't leaving until she knew Theo was safe.

She paced up and down the edge of the road, her eyes glued to the crash site, willing Theo to reappear. Hadn't he heard the sirens? Didn't he know the cavalry had arrived? He could come out now, let the emergency services crew do their jobs.

Finally, he emerged.

'Theo, thank God.' Molly hurried to his side and threw her arms around him.

Over Theo's shoulder Molly saw a paramedic heading towards them. He'd obviously seen Theo emerge from the debris and assumed he was injured.

'I'm fine,' Theo said when the paramedic touched him on the arm. 'I wasn't caught up in the accident. I'm a doctor. There's a young woman trapped in the rubble and I went in to see if I could help her.'

'She's alive?'

Theo nodded. 'Barely.' He kept his voice low and Molly could see him looking around the crowd, searching for Josh.

'Her boyfriend is in one of the ambulances,' Molly told him.

Theo nodded again and gestured to a policeman and called him over. He didn't let go of Molly—was he supporting her or did he need reassurance as well? Molly tucked herself against his side, not willing to be separated from him.

'The car has pinned her against the wall of the building. She's trapped by her legs.' Theo addressed the paramedic. 'The car seems to have missed her abdomen and vital organs but I suspect she's losing blood from somewhere. Her pulse and respiration are elevated and she's drifting in and out of consciousness. It's going to be difficult and time-consuming to free her. She might not survive long enough to be freed and if she does then the process of releasing her could still prove fatal. Falling blood pressure is a major concern. I think we should have an air ambulance on standby. She's going to need to be transferred to a major hospital in Brisbane or Sydney.'

Theo turned to the policeman. 'And the veranda will have to be secured before we move the car.'

The policeman nodded. 'We've called in the engineers and the fire brigade will try to stabilise the structure while we wait. We need to clear the area now.'

'Come on, you need to get warmed up.' Theo was speaking to Molly now. She was still tucked against his side but she hadn't realised she was shaking. She hadn't realised she was cold.

Theo took her hand in his and led her away from the chaos and the trauma. There was nothing more they could do now. It was going to take some time to plan, prepare and complete the rescue and retrieval and emergency services were now in charge. 'Will you come back to my place?'

Molly nodded. She didn't want to be alone. She needed company. She needed to hold Theo, to feel that he was okay, unharmed and in one piece.

She held tight to Theo's hand. She thought it might be the only thing keeping her upright. Adrenalin continued to course through her system, making her legs shaky. Fear tainted her voice as she asked, 'What on earth did you think you were doing, going into that situation?'

Theo looked at her for a moment before he responded. 'There might have been something I could do. I had to try. All I could think of was what if that had been you trapped in there? Alone. Injured. What if I could make a difference? Imagine how terrifying it would be to be alone in a situation like that.'

Molly didn't have to imagine. She knew the level of fear. 'But it *was* you in there—I can imagine. What if you hadn't come out again?'

'But I did. I'm fine. Now we just have to hope that Bree will be too.'

'I need a shower,' Theo said as he unlocked his front door. He was still holding Molly's hand. He hadn't let go since they'd left the accident site, and she hadn't wanted him to. He stepped into the bathroom, taking her with him, and turned the taps on, running the shower.

Molly sat on the closed toilet lid as Theo fiddled with the taps, adjusting the temperature. She looked properly at him now and realised he was filthy. She hadn't noticed, she hadn't been paying attention to his clothes, she'd just been grateful that he was okay.

The bathroom was filling with steam, the fog reminiscent of the cloud of dust that had engulfed the crash site. Molly shivered as the memory tore back into her consciousness.

'I think you should have a shower too,' Theo said. 'It'll be the quickest way to warm you up.'

Molly could barely speak but she wasn't cold any more—she was numb. Frightened. Terrified. She still hadn't recovered from the idea that she could have lost him. She was well aware that he was leaving, which meant she was going to lose him in one form, but losing him to Sydney was better than losing him altogether.

Theo took her hand and helped her to her feet. As the mirror clouded with fog he began to gently remove her clothes. He unzipped her dress and Molly lifted her arms, letting him slide it over her head. The room was warm, thick with steam and moisture. He squatted down, running his hands down the length of her legs to undo the laces on her sneakers. She lifted one foot, then the other, as he slid her shoes from her feet.

His hands were on her hips now, warm against

her skin. A tingle of awareness and anticipation surged through her as Theo slipped his fingers under the elastic of her underwear and pushed it from her hips. He stood up and moved behind her to undo the clasp on her bra. He wrapped his arms around her and his hands cupped her breasts. Her breasts were full and heavy, already changed by her pregnancy. His fingers ran over her nipple and it peaked immediately under his touch. Her breasts were far more sensitive than normal too. Another side-effect of her raging hormones.

Molly's knees trembled and Theo held her up with one arm around her waist. He half lifted her and helped her into the shower.

Molly pressed a hand into the tiled wall to support herself and let the hot water run over her as she watched Theo get undressed. His clothes were filthy and one leg on his cotton chinos was torn. In contrast his chest, when he removed his shirt, was smooth and tanned and clean. He kicked off his shoes and stepped out of his ripped trousers and underwear in one movement.

When he was naked Molly reached her hand out to him and pulled him under the water with her.

He cupped his hand at the back of her neck, sliding his fingers through her hair, and pulled her to him. He bent his head and covered her lips with his. His lips were soft and Molly sighed and leant into him as she opened her mouth. She parted her lips and let his tongue explore her mouth.

Her hands skimmed over his naked buttocks. They were tight and firm and warm under her fingers. She pulled him towards her, pressing her stomach against his erection. She wanted him closer. Needed him closer.

Her breasts, plump and ripe, flattened against his chest. She arched her back and her breasts sprang free. Theo cradled one in the palm of his hand as he ran his thumb over her nipple. A throaty moan escaped from her lips as she tipped her head back and broke their kiss.

She reached down and wrapped her hand around his shaft. It throbbed under her touch, springing to life, infused with blood. She could feel every beat of his heart repeated under her fingers.

He ducked his head and took one breast in his mouth as Molly clung to him. His tongue flicked over her nipple, sending needles of desire shooting down to the junction between her thighs. It felt amazing but she wanted more. She was desperate for more.

She held onto his shoulders and arched her

back as she thrust her hips towards him. His fingers slid inside her, rubbing the sensitive bud that nestled between her thighs. Her knees were shaking. She was incapable of thinking. She was far too busy feeling. Her body was a quivering mass of nerve endings, her senses heightened, touch, taste and smell being flooded with information courtesy of Theo's lips and fingers.

'I don't think I can stand any longer,' she panted. She was barely able to find the breath to speak. 'You'll have to hold me.'

He scooped her up in one easy motion and she spread her legs, eager to welcome him. She felt the tip of his erection nudge between her legs as she wrapped her thighs around his waist. She heard him sigh as he plunged into her.

She enveloped him as he thrust into her warmth.

God, that felt good.

She moaned as he pushed deeper.

'I'm not hurting you?'

'No.' The word was a sigh, one syllable on a breath of air.

She closed her eyes as she rode him, bucking her hips against his, her back arched. She was completely oblivious to everything except the feel of him inside her as she offered herself to him. His face was buried into her neck and she tipped her head back as he thrust into her, bringing them to their peak.

'Oh, God, Molly, that feels incredible.'

Hearing her name on his lips was her undoing. Her name had never sounded so sweet and she had never felt so desired. She gave herself up to him and as he exploded into her she joined him, quivering in his arms as she climaxed.

He kissed her forehead and her lips and held her close until she stopped shaking.

Molly was lying in Theo's arms. She was emotionally spent from the events of the evening and physically exhausted after their lovemaking, but she couldn't sleep. She lay in the dark and listened to Theo breathing. It was a sound she didn't think she would ever tire of.

She didn't want to lose him. How would she find her happily ever after once he was gone? Would their baby fill that void? She didn't think so. A baby and a partner were two very different things. She'd told Theo she was happy being single, that she was working on herself, that she didn't want a partner, but she knew now that she wanted Theo. She still didn't want to be married but that didn't rule out something more serious with Theo.

She thought she might be falling in love with

him. That was unexpected but not as frightening as she might have once thought.

Should she tell him how she was feeling? No. She didn't want to be the one to take the risk. She'd told Daniel she loved him once. He hadn't said it back. She wasn't prepared to go through that pain again.

'Are you awake?' she asked.

'Yes.'

'Are you thinking about the accident? About Bree?'

'In a roundabout way. I'm thinking about our baby. About how life is short. What if something had happened to me today? I know you were worried. I should have thought about that before I rushed into trying to be a hero. If something had gone wrong I would have left you and the baby alone. I know you said you're happy to be a single mother but I don't want to be an absent father. I want to be around for our child. My father lived in the same house as me and I barely saw him. I can't stand the thought of being in Sydney if you and our child are here.'

Molly held her breath and hoped he wasn't going to ask her to move again. She didn't want to say goodbye to him, but she knew he would be gone in less than a week. And that was her doing. She had said she wouldn't move to Sydney. She'd told him she wanted to make her own decisions. But now she thought that perhaps they could have compromised, but she wasn't sure how or what she could have done. How were they going to make long-distance parenting work?

'What if I stayed here?' Theo said.

'Here?'

'Yes.'

Her heart had leapt with hope at his suggestion until reality swiftly kicked in. 'But you're supposed to be taking over your mother's business.'

'I might be able to do that from here.'

'Why would you do that?'

'Being around for my child is more important than living in Sydney. If you want to live in Byron Bay, that's where I'll be. I'm not prepared to walk away from my responsibility to my child.'

She had been terrified that she was going to lose him tonight when he'd disappeared under the building. She couldn't imagine her life without him in it. She'd be happy if he stayed but what would that mean for them?

'And what about us?' she asked. The baby was tying them together but what would have happened to them if she weren't pregnant? Was it a relationship that could have survived or would it have run its course with time?

'I'm not saying we have to be in a relationship, although I acknowledge we will have one of sorts because of our child, but what if we could have more than a summer romance?' he said. 'A proper relationship.'

'But not marriage?' Marriage was still a step too far. She wasn't prepared to give up her independence and that was how she viewed marriage. From her experience it wasn't a partnership. It involved compromise, she understood that, but from her experience one person always compromised more than the other. Theo hadn't said he loved her. If she let herself fall in love with him, she knew she would be the one to compromise. She would be the one with everything to lose.

'No,' he agreed. 'We can keep seeing each other but without pressure, without expectation. We need to find a way forward. Together. But we don't need to figure it all out tonight. We've got eight months to work out how we're going to navigate this. I just need to know if it's an idea you'd consider. If you'd be okay if I stayed?'

'Yes,' she said. 'I would.' She'd be more than okay with that. 'I think we should see what happens.'

'My mother is back in the country tomorrow after her conference. I'll call her tomorrow night and put my proposal to her.'

# CHAPTER TEN

'I CAN'T BELIEVE you've done this.' Theo was on the phone to his mother. He'd called to discuss the possibility of him staying on in Byron Bay, he hadn't mentioned Molly or the pregnancy—that was a conversation best had face to face—but she had completely blindsided him with news of her own. And the news wasn't good. 'You didn't think to tell me?'

'No. It was my decision and it was too good an opportunity to pass up.'

'When are you going to tell the staff?' he asked.

'I thought you could do it tomorrow before you come back to Sydney. You won't be staying in Byron Bay now.'

'You want *me* to tell them?'

'Yes. Making tough calls is part and parcel of management. If you're going to take over the practice one day you need to be able to have these conversations. To take responsibility. Think of it as a learning experience.'

Theo wasn't sure he wanted the responsibility or the experience. In his opinion he was going to be the bearer of bad tidings without having any input into the decision. But he knew there wasn't much he could do. The decision had been made.

All his plans were unravelling.

Theo felt sick. His mother's news had cost him a night with Molly. He couldn't face her last night, not with this decision hanging over his head, and he'd made an excuse, told her a lie, and now he was hoping she didn't find out. He knew a lack of trust was a deal breaker for her.

He was the first person to arrive for the fortnightly Monday morning staff meeting. He wanted to make sure he had time to gather his thoughts and run through his announcement. No, not his announcement, his mother's.

He smiled at Molly when she arrived, only marginally late, but his smile felt forced. He then avoided looking at her, knowing he would have difficulty getting through the announcement if he caught her eye. He knew he would see disappointment in her expression.

'Most of you know that my mother, Lian Chin, is the owner of Pacific Coast Clinics. She has some news that she has asked me to pass on. It affects all of you. Some of you know that this clinic hasn't been performing as well as expected recently and Lian has decided that the Byron Bay clinic is no longer a required part of the business portfolio, and she has sold the property and is going to offer the practice as an ongoing concern to any potential purchasers.'

'What? We're losing our jobs?'

He could tell Gemma was incensed, but part of him was glad that it was Gemma who had spoken up. He wasn't game to meet Molly's gaze yet. 'The clinic will be offered as an ongoing concern, but the purchaser would have to find new premises. This site has been sold to developers.' He knew that financially the sale of the building made sense. It was a large landholding, on a corner site in the centre of town. But the decision did not sit well with him morally. 'We're hoping to find someone who wants to take the practice and the staff on.'

'And if you don't?'

'We've got three months before the site needs to be vacated. I'm hopeful that will give everyone time to find another job if we don't find a buyer for the clinic.' Theo's stomach felt as if it were lined with lead. He couldn't believe he was imparting this news and, by the look on the faces of everyone in the room, nether could they. 'I'm sorry, there's not much more I can tell you, but I'm happy to answer any questions that you might have, if I can.'

The room was silent. Nobody had anything to say. They were all stunned. Theo had been feeling included, feeling comfortable, as a member of staff, but that had all changed within the space of a few minutes, several sentences and one decision.

'I'll let you discuss this news among yourselves. You're welcome to ask me anything you need to throughout the day.' He thought the best course of action would be to leave the room and give them freedom to discuss the announcement without him present but as he headed for the door he saw Molly rise from her chair.

'Theo.' She had followed him from the room.

She closed the door behind her. 'What the hell was that all about?'

'I'm sorry, Molly.'

'You're sorry? We're going to lose our jobs and you're sorry! How long have you known about this?'

'I only found out last night. When I called Mum to discuss staying here.'

Molly laughed. 'Really. Did you ever actually intend to stay here?'

Theo frowned. 'Of course. We talked about it.'

'We talked about a lot of things. We talked about the practice and the issues it was facing. We gave you suggestions. Did you even discuss those with your mother or was this a done deal?'

'We discussed it, but she felt that selling the building made the most sense financially.'

'I thought you agreed medicine was about more than money.'

'I do. But this was her decision. I'm as upset by this as you are.'

'I don't think so. This doesn't affect you nearly as much. It's not your livelihood at stake. You have a job in Sydney.'

'What do you mean? I'm staying here.'

'Not on my account, you're not.'

'What does that mean?'

'You know how much this job means to me. This place. These people. I won't be manipulated into moving to Sydney. I can't believe you've done this to me.'

'I haven't done anything to you. And no one is asking you to move to Sydney. I was going to stay here. Why would I do that if I knew there was going to be no job? For either of us.'

'I don't think you should stay here. I think you should go back to Sydney. I think our relationship, for want of a better word, is done,' she said before she spun around and walked off, leaving him standing alone in the corridor.

The sun was shining on Sydney Harbour and it was a picture-perfect summer's day, but Theo was oblivious to his surroundings as he made his way across the city. His heart ached. He'd lost everything. Molly blamed him and he couldn't argue with her. In her eyes he'd taken everything from her and having him in her life was not enough of a consolation prize. He wasn't wanted.

He kept his head down as he walked through the clinic to his mother's office. He wasn't in the mood to make polite small talk with any of the staff. He was frustrated, heartbroken and angry. He knocked on Lian's door, his irritation manifesting in short sharp taps, loud and unapologetic. His mother owed him some more information.

'Why didn't you tell me you'd had an offer on the property before I went up to Byron?' he asked, barely able to manage a cordial greeting before launching into the root of his aggravation.

'Because I hadn't. The offer only came through once you were already there.'

'You still could have told me,' he argued. 'I thought you wanted me to look at options to make the clinic profitable and I thought we'd come up with some good ideas.'

'Many of those suggestions had merit,' Lian agreed, 'but some would have required quite a bit of capital investment. Once I got the offer to sell that made the most sense from a financial perspective as well as a time perspective. It was a lot of money tied up in the land. The site was worth far more as a development site. It didn't make financial sense to keep it.'

*Try telling that to the staff*, Theo felt like saying, though he knew that opinion wouldn't do him any favours.

'Can I ask why you bought the practice to begin with? Did it make financial sense at the time?' he asked.

'I wanted to expand, and I looked to invest in Byron Bay as it was a growth area, and I thought it might be a good option for retirement, but then I realised it's just a bit too far away to keep an eye on easily and your father and I decided we didn't actually want to retire, or even semi-retire, to Byron Bay. We like Sydney, our friends are here and it's convenient. It was a mistake to buy it.'

Theo's eyebrows shot up.

'What is it?' Lian asked when she saw his expression.

Theo shook his head. 'I've never heard you say you've made a mistake.'

'I've made a few,' Lian replied. 'But I hope I've learnt something from each one. If you can fix it or learn from it, it can be a positive. A mistake isn't a problem unless you repeat it.'

And that was when Theo realised that he'd made a mistake. And he'd made it twice.

Twice he'd walked away from Molly.

He'd let her down, unintentionally it had to be said, but that didn't change the fact that he hadn't supported her. He hadn't fought for her and he was ashamed of himself.

She'd pushed him away because he'd broken her trust and he couldn't blame her for that. He recognised that, for all her talk of independence, it was her fear of being let down that had led her to strive for that in the first instance. If she didn't depend on anyone she wouldn't be disappointed. His fears of rejection, of not being deemed good enough, had caused him to walk away, believing she didn't want him, only Molly had taken that to believe that he wasn't someone she could rely on. When what she really wanted was to be able to depend on someone. On him.

He should have fought harder for her.

He should have stayed.

His mother's words resonated with him. About

mistakes but also about retirement. About finding somewhere to slow down. About Byron Bay.

That was where he should be. He'd found peace, acceptance and happiness there. With Molly. He could imagine growing old there. With Molly. And that was where he wanted to be, not in forty years' time but right now. With Molly.

The woman he loved.

He loved her.

He should never have left her.

Was it possible that together they could overcome their fears? That they could be stronger together?

Was it too late to win her back? Too late to tell her how he felt? Too late to make amends?

He had to try. He'd already lost everything. There was nothing more to lose.

He knew what he had to do.

'I have a proposal for you,' he said to his mother.

Molly stood beneath the lighthouse, a solitary figure, alone with her thoughts. She was up before sunrise, unable to sleep, but her eyes were closed now. She was leaning on the railing, facing east, listening to the waves crashing onto the rocks below her. The sound reminded her of Theo. Rolling waves were the soundtrack of their lovemaking.

She opened her eyes, looking for something to distract her, something to take her mind off Theo, but the ocean was empty and the horizon was only just beginning to glow.

It was Christmas Eve and he'd been gone for almost a week. Her heart ached. He'd broken it, smashed it, but she would have to find a way to deal with that, to deal with him, because even though he was gone, even though she had sent him away, there was no escape. He was the father of her unborn child and she knew that would connect them for ever.

Had she expected too much from him?

She hadn't expected to fall in love and that was when her expectations had changed. She'd said she wanted independence but then she'd changed her mind but hadn't told him. That was hardly his fault.

A life with Theo had, for a brief time, been what she wanted but depending on someone else frightened her, so much that she'd taken the first opportunity presented to her to push him away. By accusing him of letting her down, she'd sacrificed their relationship for her independence at the first hurdle.

Had she been too quick to judge? Should she have tried harder to work things through?

Had she made a mistake?

Maybe, but now she was stuck with the consequences of her actions. Stuck with having to co-parent with Theo without being with him.

She'd acted hastily and she was as much to blame for the situation as he was. But that didn't lessen her heartache.

Would her heart ache so much if she weren't still in love with him? Unfortunately for her she couldn't turn love off like a tap. She had banished Theo but she couldn't banish her feelings and now she'd just have to find a way to manage. Given time, she might be able to do that.

She had thirty-five weeks until her due date. That might be enough time.

Or it might not.

With a little effort she pushed thoughts of Theo to one side. There were more pressing issues to deal with right now. She needed to get on with her life. The future she'd pictured briefly with Theo had changed completely. She needed to do something about finding a new job. She couldn't afford to wait. She was going to be a single mother; she needed to be settled into a job before she had the baby. She needed her new employer to find her invaluable. Her priority had to be her baby. Her heartache would ease and she'd eventually work out how to co-parent with Theo.

She turned south, looking away from the horizon towards the road leading to the lighthouse, imagining, over the sound of the waves and the seagulls, that someone was calling her name. She didn't expect to see anyone, she assumed it must be a trick of the wind, so she was surprised to see a familiar figure jogging up the path.

Her heart rate quickened as her body betrayed her.

Theo.

He slowed his pace as he approached her. Was he unsure of his reception? His dark eyes showed signs of fatigue—had he been sleeping poorly too? She curled her hand into a fist, forcing herself not to reach out to him, not to smooth the worry lines from his face. She wasn't the person to console him any more.

He stopped in front of her. Just out of reach. His eyes dark with apprehension.

'What are you doing here?' she asked.

'Looking for you.' His answer was matter-of-fact but his voice was soft and filled with longing and Molly's heart lifted with hope.

He was looking at her closely, his gaze intense, and she felt the familiar and not unpleasant sensation of her insides melting, turning to warm treacle. 'How are you?'

Molly almost laughed. His question was so brief, so minuscule compared to her feelings. She was devastated over what she'd lost, feeling sorry for herself and also annoyed that her first reaction to seeing Theo had been pleasure, but she didn't tell him that. 'I'm fine.' She could do brief.

'And the baby?'

His question brought a half-smile to her lips. 'The baby is the size of a sesame seed.' She was only five weeks pregnant. She knew the baby would be getting facial features now—eyes and a nose—it was developing into a tiny human, but it was still tiny.

'I know, but I've missed a week.' He shrugged. His tone wasn't accusatory, which was just as well. His banishment was his own fault. 'It's felt like a lifetime.'

She heard the heartache in his words but he had only himself to blame for that. Her heart was aching too. She didn't want to cover old ground so she repeated her question. 'What are you doing here?'

'I need to talk to you.'

'I'm not sure there's anything we need to discuss.' Her heart was bruised, her pride dented, her trust broken and the pain made her tone sharp.

'Please,' he begged her, 'can we sit down? Can you give me five minutes? It's important.'

The sun was only just starting to peek above the horizon. Molly had nowhere else to be and, she couldn't deny it, suddenly nowhere else she wanted to be. She nodded and let Theo lead her to a bench against the lighthouse wall. She sat and folded her arms across her stomach, keeping her distance, knowing if she let him touch her she'd be in danger of believing anything he said.

He reached for her but withdrew his hands as she crossed her arms. 'It may make no difference to what happens next, but it's important that you know this,' he said. 'I know you think I colluded with my mother, but I promise you she made all the decisions regarding the practice. I'm not trying to shift the blame to her. I'm telling you the truth. She didn't consult me about the sale. I knew nothing of it until twelve hours before I told all the staff.'

Hope died in Molly's heart. Had he come back just to rehash business matters? She admitted to herself she'd been wanting more, hoping for something personal. Hoping he'd missed her as much as she'd missed him. She sighed inwardly. He'd asked about the baby—was that the best she could expect? 'Why hadn't your mother told you about the sale earlier?'

'Apparently she only received that offer from the developers when she was overseas at the conference.'

'And you believe her?'

Theo nodded. 'I've seen the emails.'

'Why didn't you say anything to me as soon as you found out? Why didn't you give me some warning?'

'I didn't know how to tell you. I was afraid of what it might mean.'

'Did you even try to talk her out of it? We came up with lots of options—did you even discuss any of those with her? Did you try to fight for us?'

Theo nodded. 'I did but the reality was the offer to sell was too good to refuse. I agreed with her on that.'

Molly opened her mouth to interject.

'But I disagreed with her next move of giving up the practice entirely,' Theo continued, as if knowing what Molly was about to say. 'The town needs the clinic. She should have considered that and realised that not every health practitioner wants to run their own practice. She could have handled that better. This whole situation has taught me a few more things about my mother and myself. It was a unilateral decision and when I questioned her she told me it was hers to make. I know she intends for me to take over the business one day but the way this decision was made makes me question whether she will ever really let go. Whether the clinics will ever be mine to run as I choose. But I think I have found a solution.'

'Which is?' Molly's voice was flat. She was going through the motions, feigning polite interest, responding to Theo's words, when in reality she wanted to know if he'd really come back just to talk about work.

'I'm going to take over the Byron Bay clinic. I'll need to find another site but I'm going to keep it going. My way. Our way.'

'Our way?'

'I understand none of this might make any difference to how you feel about me, but I want to be here. I want to be where my child is. I don't want to be a part-time father. I'm not walking away again. I want to be here, with you. I want us to do this together.'

'Do what exactly?' Molly asked.

'Work together.'

'You want me to work in the clinic? Your new clinic?' What was wrong with men? Which part of independence didn't he get? Did he think that she would be grateful to have a job? She would, that much was true, but she wasn't going to work for him.

'I know how important your job is to you,' he said. 'How much you love the town. You want financial independence, job security and to be able to stay here. I think my solution gives us both what we're looking for.'

'But you'll still control my fate. My employment. I don't want to be controlled by anyone.'

Theo shook his head. 'I want you to work in the clinic if that's what you choose, but not as an employee. I want to make you a partner in the business. I want you to have the independence you need.'

'A partnership?'

Theo nodded.

'I can't afford to buy into a practice,' she told him. A business partnership was appealing but she didn't even have money for a lawyer to draw up a contract, let alone money to start a business.

'It will be my gift to you.'

Molly frowned. 'A gift? You'd do that for me?' She tilted her head as she considered him. What did he want in exchange? she wondered.

'Yes. I want you to know you can trust me, but I thought a physical commitment would give you protection, a guarantee. No one will be able to take it away from you.'

Theo's eyes were dark and solemn, almost begging her to believe him. To trust him. Could she? She wanted to—desperately. 'Is that all you want?'

He shook his head. 'Not quite.'

She knew there would be more. There was always more.

'I want to raise our child together, not as two single parents but as a couple. I want to be in a relationship with you, if you'll have me. I made a mistake leaving here. I made a mistake leaving you. I don't want to give up on you, on us. I want to give you the world and I want to make a life with you. I want a family, people I can love without reservation. I love you, Molly.'

'You love me?' That wasn't the addition she was expecting. Once upon a time, just ten days ago, it was the extra piece she was hoping for but she'd let go of that dream. Now her heart leapt with hope.

'I love you.'

She heard the catch of emotion in his voice as he repeated his words. He loved her.

Could she possibly have everything she'd dared to dream of?

'I love you,' he repeated for the third time. He

shook his head as if he couldn't believe it himself. 'I've never said that to anyone before.'

'Have you never been in love?' she asked.

'Once. With an amazing girl,' he said, and Molly steeled herself for what was coming next. 'She was bright and beautiful and she could light up a room. And I'm still in love with her. It's you, Molly. It's always been you.'

Molly's heart soared as she broke into a smile. She'd almost convinced herself that she didn't need anyone, that she didn't need him, but she knew that wasn't true. He loved her. And she loved him.

She had sacrificed their relationship for her independence only to realise that wasn't what she wanted after all. But now Theo was offering her everything. Independence along with a commitment and, best of all, his love, and she knew she wanted to make the same promise to Theo. She wanted to be his.

She reached for his hands as she said, 'I love you too. I didn't want to fall in love, but I can't resist you. I can't live without you. When you went into that collapsed building and I thought I might lose you that was the worst moment of my life. I realised I'd fallen in love with you, but then I thought you let me down and I convinced myself that I was better off without you in my life.

I jumped to conclusions and I'm sorry. I'd been so afraid that you'd let me down that I made myself believe you had, just to prove myself right, just to make my expectations real, but I've been miserable. I've missed you. I've missed you so much.' She paused before finally uttering the words she needed to say. 'I love you too.'

Theo was beaming, his gorgeous grin stretching widely across his beautiful face. The morning sun fell on his face, turning his skin golden and making his dark eyes shine. He gathered her to him, wrapping his arms around her, and Molly lost herself in his embrace.

'What do you think?' he asked. 'Let's spend Christmas Day together and the next day and the next, and then we can celebrate a new year together and create a life for ourselves here where we can be happy. We'll have our work, our family, we'll have each other. Will you be my partner? In work and life?'

Molly sat back. She needed to clarify exactly what he was asking. 'Does your version of family look like a traditional one? I will be your partner, we will be a family, but I don't want to get married. Not yet. Maybe not ever. But that doesn't mean I don't love you. I want to be with you. I don't want anyone else, but marriage isn't for me. Can you live with that?'

'I won't deny that I would marry you in a heartbeat,' Theo replied, 'but, married or not, it won't affect how much I love you or our child. Married or not, I will still try to be the best partner, the best father, I can be. I'll be happy if I can wake up beside you every day. I want to spend the rest of my life with you. I love you and a wedding ring won't change that. I will love you just the same.'

The lighthouse towered above them, but Molly was oblivious to its beauty. All her focus was on the man in front of her. The love of her life. She was smiling now as she pulled Theo towards her.

'Then, yes, let's do this. Today, tomorrow and the next day. You and me together,' she said, before she kissed him with all her heart and soul. 'I love you.'

* * * * *

*If you enjoyed this story, check out these other great reads from Emily Forbes*

Rescued by the Australian GP
Ali and the Rebel Doc
Marriage Reunion in the ER
The Perfect Mother for His Son

*All available now!*